S0-BYR-803

The Silent Partner
Ellen Gold
Chris Blanno
Susan York

STRAUS

A JOAN KAHN BOOK

STRAUS

by

Anders Bodelsen

Translated from the Danish by

Nadia Christensen and Alexander Taylor

HARPER & ROW, PUBLISHERS

New York, Evanston, San Francisco, London

A Harper Novel of Suspense

FIRST EDITION

Designed by Janice Stern

Library of Congress Cataloging in Publication Data

Bodelsen, Anders, 1937–
    Straus.

    I. Title.
PZ4.B6658St4   [PT8176.1Z.034]   839.8'1'374   73–4140
ISBN 0-06-010402-3

STRAUS

February

February Eleventh

On the whole, the twenty-sixth of January was like any other day in the life of Denmark's second-best crime writer, but before *his* day ended he had committed a murder.

Well, that's half the battle. This may end up being my ninth novel, and I'm following the principles I've always followed: Catch the reader's attention as soon as possible. Make a promise, then it doesn't matter so much if it takes a little while before you keep it. Let's look at my first sentence. (But now some devil or other has already got me out of the novel and I catch myself wondering if I'll ever get to finish it. Maybe it would be a good idea to begin all over again, begin with the figure one—this figure one that has always frightened me because it means months of difficulty ahead, work that can never be seen in its entirety before it is finished, and that never turns out exactly the way you imagined at the beginning.) Where was I? Oh, yes, let's look at the first sentence. It raises suspense in two ways. The first is obvious and actually less exciting—at least it's the most ordinary and more commonly used. Dear Reader, it says, have a little patience; all beginnings are difficult, but you will get your murder, I promise you. Not only in the course of the book (in the course of the book perhaps you'll get several), but in the course of the first day of the man the book's about. And the first day eats up two chapters at the most. Before then,

I promise you, we'll be right in the midst of things. But give me a chance to warm up a little first. After all, it's most exciting when we wait a little while for the murder. It will come, I promise you.

Note that it was the somewhat trite and fairly obvious promise which I managed to plant in the first sentence (sometimes I'm satisfied with planting the promise in the first paragraph and sometimes I wait a whole chapter; but it is, after all, a good rule to hold out the prospect of something immediately, in order to, so to speak, grab the reader by the lapels right away and keep holding him if you can). The second promise I like better. Who do I promise will undoubtedly commit a murder before the reader loses his patience? Not just anybody. Not . . . What shall we call him? I had thought of calling the main character in my unfinished ninth, which lies in my suitcase but which never will be written now, Anthon Bendix (common last name, Bendix), and I can't find anything better in a hurry, so I'll keep it as the only memento of a book I carried out only as far as a quite unpromising prelude: Anthon Bendix, then. Good initials. They'll inevitably give the critics something to think about. The last sentence having anything to do with the story went: Not just anybody . . . and I continue: Not crime writer Anthon Bendix. No, Denmark's *second-best* crime writer. For the more or less observant reader, the adjective implies yet another promise. Why isn't he just good or mediocre or poor? Or possibly the best (or, to make it complete, the worst)? Why precisely the second-best? The answer can only be: Because there is someone who is better than he, and this fact will play a part.

Promises, promises—you have to give promises, and then you have to try to keep them.

I sit watching the typing element on my I.B.M. typewriter—it moves faster than the eye can perceive. I'm writing the same way, faster than I can think, and when I woke up this morning I had decided to follow my usual procedure—narrate very calmly from the beginning and never lose the over-all view. My slightly pedantic style by which I've acquired so many readers and so many critics. If you watch carefully you can actually see the typing element move, after all. But perhaps it won't be my lot to write more than the eight crime

4

stories that have earned me my reputation and money. I sit here feeling as if I've been set on rails and someone has given me a good shove. I've only been writing for an hour—no, forty-five minutes at the most—and I've already (now the metaphors are skidding) slid off the track. No, I haven't slid off the track, I've only slid onto the wrong track, and maybe that has something to do with the fact that the first sentence, which I'm so proud of, wasn't actually the first thing that I wrote down at all. I started by writing a date (as if this were to be a novel in diary form!) and thereby I indicated to myself that this would not be my ninth, but something else—maybe just some notes rattled down to get the long row of identically sunny days to pass while I pull myself together and try to figure out what I am going to do. Maybe the idea was that the dates would be taken out and replaced by chapter titles of some sort as I gradually got a grip on the material. But I've usually had a good grip on the material even before I began —that was, among other reasons, why they called me a pedant. (And that was why I became good enough . . . to . . . to . . . yes, now I find it hard even to finish a sentence, but let me just say: earn a lot of money. Because readers like things to be orderly, too.) Have I got a grip on my material now? Yes and no. All these private reflections will have to go if this is to be the ninth in the series. But one could, of course, begin a new series. Didn't some composer or other discover that all the Greats died after their ninth—symphony? So he tried calling one of his symphonies something else, and that way he managed to get started on number ten, but he died in the middle of it. Mahler, I think it was. Anyway, it's not dying I'm afraid of now. Or is it? No, rather it's never to get any further than number eight. My God, this is some paragraph I'm writing; and now I've forgotten again what it was that I was getting at.

Yes, all these digressions are of course only scribbled down for the sake of my private enjoyment, and they must come out before I send the book to . . . a new unfinished and unfinishable sentence. Who, for Christ's sake, will I send this to? Can I send it home and have it published under a pseudonym? Would they publish it under my own name? How would I get the money down here? Well, there's time to think about all this. If nothing else, I got the first sentence down on paper, and that's quite a bit. Let's consider today a warm-up and begin seriously tomorrow. Another long day of sunshine and I haven't the faintest idea what to do with myself. The day's total result: the first sentence, and then I sped off the track. But tomorrow I'll write the first sentence again, and then I'll try to keep on the track which, in spite of everything, I do have in my head. Don't think I've changed so much that I don't have a fairly precise synopsis because otherwise I wouldn't have sat down at the typewriter. Today there was a little technical breakdown; tomorrow I'll know this new element of risk and be on my guard against it. But it's still morning, and what now?

One could, of course . . .

New paragraph. A slight pressure on a button and the typing element (not the paper) jerks into place. A slight pressure on the tabulator, and the predetermined indentation takes place. I'm used to an electric typewriter, though my machine at home was a slightly less advanced model; this one still has keys, but the main thing is that the lines shift without hand power, a little finger power is the only thing necessary. So all that's lacking is to be able to touch-type with all ten fingers. But you can't teach an old dog new tricks, and until this book (?) I thought, in spite of everything, so slowly, or so much—or whatever you'd say—that the tempos of my fingers and my head were more or less the same. Is it a good or a bad sign that now I suddenly wish I could write faster? That my thoughts are always a couple of sentences ahead of my fingers? I have the feeling that some people will say I have at last learned how to write. Surprises for myself, too, along the way. Slightly less planning, slightly more . . . Excuse these dots, I think myself they're a bad habit, but my fingers want to do something, even when I'm thinking, for a change. The word I hesitated to write down was: inspiration. That's a word you should let others apply. (How difficult it is to think about the critics all the time. I wonder whether Straus feels the same way. Well, now he has popped up; he really doesn't belong here, but in the novel. I must try to keep Straus a little in check. I can already see that he has a tendency to pop up in all sorts of places where he doesn't belong.)

6

I'm using too many parentheses today; I'll have to watch that. My paragraphs are too long. And in the bargain I think I'm writing pretty short sentences; this staccato style is one of the worst I know. I have a feeling that the new typewriter tempts me to end my sentences prematurely. That's right, put the blame on the typewriter.

At last a proper paragraph, neither (notice I used a comma instead of a period; that's more like the style of the old ones, the eight) too long nor too short. And now, in order not to use another parenthesis: Stay away from all these interpolations.

I've just looked at my watch, and what a catastrophe—it's only ten o'clock. I got up from the breakfast table at nine; I've only written for an hour. I look at the typewritten pages and see that there are four of them the usual 8½ × 11 size beside my typewriter—surely I've made headway. Oh hell, actually I've only got one sentence of the novel down. But it is a catastrophe because I slept ten hours last night, I'm completely rested, and I don't know what I'll find to do if I don't keep on writing. Today I'm like a barber who snips his scissors in the air while waiting for customers. Write. Write about anything. I've already written about my typewriter, the typing element whose movements you must be alert to follow—I forgot to say it's a large I.B.M. I rented and that it's a very delicate olive-green color, somehow very professional—but I can certainly continue by letting my glance glide from the typewriter along the extension cord and into my bungalow. The door is open. The maid has been there and taken away my breakfast tray and made my bed and hung up the towels in the bathroom. Actually it's a good place for a writer I've found here. Someone sees to it that you get something to eat, the place is cleaned up after you, they call to wake you in the morning at the time you have requested, and they also arrange for someone to bring a typewriter you can rent. I haven't even had to go into the city to get paper. It's a good place—in a way I wish that we . . . or at least I had found it long ago. I could imagine having Straus work in a place like this part of the year. It would partially explain his fantastic productivity. Also the quality, in a way, for naturally you work better when the sun is shining, and you're sitting under a large umbrella with the morning's very thin first whiskey, and your family (Straus must have a large family, which he either leaves behind or installs in another bungalow at a suitable distance) is out of the way, and there is the sound of the waves from a really large ocean, and the wind, which even at ten o'clock isn't too warm, makes the tops of the palm trees nod and keeps the mosquitoes—or whatever those little beasts are that force me to sleep under a net every night—from the beach and my terrace. Yes, it's a good place to work, and maybe everything would have gone differently and I could have written much better if I'd known about this place long ago. But at some point I had got it into my head that I could only write in my own house in Hellerup; I had got it into my head to such a degree that I didn't write a line the three weeks we were on vacation in Baunebakke.

Now it's happened again. I have to turn back a page even to recall what it was I was writing. If I feel a little disoriented today, it's probably because I'm writing so fast and it's a long time (relatively) since I last wrote. At any rate, it's not sleep I need, and it's not a question of aftereffects of sleeping pills, because that is one of the things I've got rid of in my new life. I can't sleep completely without help, but I've substituted a single thin whiskey or two for the inevitable Noludar (which became two after I'd lain awake for an hour), and the pills at least are out of my system now. What I was doing earlier, as a matter of fact, was following the extension cord from my typewriter into my bungalow. I purposely asked that an extension cord at least thirty feet long be brought along with the typewriter because I wanted to be able to move my table around the terrace freely according to sun and impulse. As a man writing by hand can move about. And why not a few words about the terrace? It has red flagstones and a balustrade which is high enough so I can sit here and write without bathing trunks and not offend anyone's modesty, but something or other makes me feel it's impossible to write stark naked, so I sit here in shorts. The red flagstones absorb a good deal of the sunlight, thereby sparing the eyes—still I wouldn't dream of working without my prescription sunglasses—so they collect a lot of heat and I can't stand to touch them with my feet, so I have my sandals on too.

Finally, my watch. The table is a little too high for the typewriter, so I've taken a couple of pillows from the bed and sit teetering on them. There is a small opening in the balustrade, and through this opening I have a glimpse of the golden beach and the very blue water. But perhaps first I should go through (though for whose enjoyment? to make the time pass?) what I have on the table.

The handsome olive-green typewriter. A bottle of whiskey and a glass, which is now empty. A thermos bucket with a lid, for icecubes, and a siphon (now I notice how little I've got away from my old style —all these pedantic details which my few and far-between supporters among the reviewers believed expressed some philosophy or other, though the truth of the matter was they were only an expression of my "personality" or simply a bad habit, which intensified when I became conscious of it). A box of Henry Clay cigars, which would have cost about two dollars apiece in Denmark. A little cigar clipper, which isn't actually used for clipping a cigar, but to bore a hole in the end of it. An ashtray containing ashes and the stump of the day's first cigar (I'm about to reach the point in the second one where it heats the lips more than is comfortable but tastes better than ever: a dilemma). The daily paper, which they bring me with breakfast, and which I try to read—that is, I try to guess at what it says in the headlines and in "Peanuts" on the back page, which, interestingly enough, is also called "Peanuts" here. While I remember it, I could eliminate my little morning walk into the vestibule of the main building with a single word. It's about time I get them to give me one of the American newspapers instead of the local one so I can see what's happening in the world. Maybe one day there will even be something about Denmark.

I've moved the umbrella, poured myself a new thin whiskey, and decided to go a little further with the story. It's too early to give up for the day; there are still two hours, or at least an hour and a half, until siesta time, and I think I'll be able to take a nap if I can get a little more done. On the whole, progress and so forth. So the first sentence indicates that the man is Denmark's second-best crime writer, that the day progressed by and large as days ordinarily progressed for our man, but also that it ended rather unusually. I concluded the sentence *his* day because, according to the plan, we will actually get a good way into the next day before the murder is committed. Another thing: I chose the date the twenty-sixth of January a bit at random, nevertheless with cold calculation because it's useful to me that it should be winter, it's useful to me that it should be January (the visit with the accountant), and so, all things considered, I decided on a winter novel this time. Of course, nobody but myself has thought about it, and there will hardly ever be others who will think about it, but with a single exception I've written my eight books alternating between summer novels and winter novels; and since I started with a summer novel (oh, lost innocence, my first novel), it works out that all my odd-numbered novels (with the exception of one that stretched out over several years) are winter novels. Variety is the spice of life, if not for others, then for the author.

Anthon Bendix (but after this we are on a last-name basis with him) had himself awakened by the answering service as usual. Before he took his cold shower and brushed his teeth, he started the coffee. At eight o'clock he was sitting at his typewriter and had lit the day's first cigar while he drank his second cup of coffee. He was alert, in fine form, and wrote quickly. He had finished three chapters of his new novel and had so much of the plot in his head that he felt certain he would be able to finish the book. It was the first novel he had written since he'd been alone in the house. The first days he had been afraid that the new situation—the empty house, the half-empty bookcases, the missing furniture, and the books fallen over on the bookshelves because Nadja had left with half of them—would create working problems, but it didn't. In many ways existence had become more complicated for him, but the divorce, as far as he could see at the moment, hadn't made it harder for him to write. On the contrary, about this time Nadja would begin stirring; soon she would be making noise in the bathroom, and finally she'd make her own breakfast and eat it while she read the newspaper, and sometimes she'd come into his room to get the telephone or borrow his lighter or some such thing, which meant a slight interruption in his concentration on his work.

She wouldn't leave him until about ten thirty, when she drove to the TV studio, and then he had the house to himself again, but by that time his earlier enthusiasm had gone, and he worked more and more slowly the rest of the morning until about noon, when he stopped working on the first draft. He then spent most of the afternoon revising the preceding day's work and retyping the pre-preceding day's.

On the twenty-sixth of January, Bendix was not disturbed. The mail dropped through the slot in the front door with a tiny plop, and he let it lie there for the moment. The telephone didn't ring once. Bendix worked well and with concentration, yet it was clear to him as he sat writing that something was wrong. Not with what he was writing now, but with the whole idea of the novel. It was a feeling he had had from the first day, but was unable to concretize. He shoved the feeling aside, but decided that during the day he'd sit down for an hour, listen to some relaxing music on his stereo, figure out what was wrong, and consider whether it could be corrected before he got so far into his work that a deal already began to be a deal.

After writing a few books, Bendix had arrived at a principle of composition which made his work easier for him. In the beginning he had written long chapters, each one of which required many days' work. Now he always wrote such short chapters that he could get through one in a single day—in fact, in less than a day—a morning was enough. This way he could make each chapter a unified whole, something he envisioned and wrote down all in one sitting; while at the same time he had a good overview of the whole novel, which he planned would consist of between eighteen and twenty-four chapters. Allowing for a reasonable number of days in which to rest, make notations, and reread the entire manuscript straight through, the time needed for the work amounted to six weeks altogether. Bendix' last five books had all been written in less than two months. It was nice to know ahead of time that the torment wouldn't last any longer than that, and it was very nice to know that every working day the book progressed at a precisely defined pace. Before Bendix went to sleep at night he always thought about the next day's work and hoped that his fed subconscious would work while he slept. Each chapter was written

11

so that it ended with a question which would be answered only if the reader went on to the next chapter. Bendix took it for granted that the reader liked the short chapters—each with its unsolved problem —as much as he did.

Much too long a paragraph. God knows whether people are interested in a crime writer's working habits. You've promised them a murder, but how much do you think you can get them to swallow with that carrot dangling in front of their noses? Well, one can always abridge it. The question is whether people even care to read about authors. Why have you made him an author? Because that's the easiest—you know him. But don't you know him too well? Aren't you about to get lost in details that are of interest only to you? You've used a composer, a TV man, an editor of a weekly, a crime reporter; but you've never dared write about . . . yes, think of Bendix now—his novel is going to be about a traveling salesman, it *is* about a traveling salesman. Could you yourself write about a traveling salesman? Certainly; you'd go and do research and collect a lot of details you could use, but still you'd only know the man from the outside. Well, that's Bendix' problem, too. That's why he sits there feeling that something is wrong with his book though it's going very nicely at the moment. He has found a couple of traits which can characterize the man. Smoking habits, the fact that he always picks up hitchhikers (which proves to be his undoing), the fact that he plays the numbers according to a system and bets between ten and fifteen dollars a week while waiting for the big win. That's Bendix' problem—but it's also yours, so you resort to writing about a crime writer. Well, nothing could be easier. But then you take the risk of going overboard—you know too much about the job and you plague the reader with all sorts of unimportant professional details. While we're on the subject of Bendix, it isn't a very good name anyway. It's short enough, even though a single-syllabled last name is and will remain the best, but it won't take the genitive. I'm already awfully tired of that apostrophe.

While he wrote, Bendix smoked the three cigars to which he had reduced his morning consumption. The night before, he had prepared the percolator to make four cups of coffee and at eleven thirty he poured the fourth. The chapter had been carefully planned in advance and there was a lot of dialogue, so the work went smoothly; yet he felt all the time that there was something fundamentally wrong. Perhaps, he thought, it's a matter of writing yourself out of the problem rather than thinking yourself out of it. He worked in a relaxed fashion and allowed himself short breaks to look out at the yard, which had been covered by snow since the end of November. The weather was so cold that the snow hadn't even melted along the walls of the house. He had brushed away a little of it with his hands to be sure that the snowdrops had sprouted. The thermometer outside the window of his working room registered ten degrees.

At exactly twelve o'clock Bendix finished the day's chapter and went into the hall, where he gathered up the day's mail. There were two bills, which he didn't even bother to open but just laid on top of the little stack of bills and notices which had collected there during the month of January. Their bills and finances in general had been Nadja's responsibility. The stack had become disconcertingly large; a few of the bills were second notices with pressing reminders for payment. He mustn't let himself put off much longer a major visit to the post office with checkbook, bills, envelopes, and money orders. Money was no problem for Bendix, but he found it bothersome that he should suddenly have to manage the economic side of his life. There was a letter from Nadja's lawyer, too—also about money problems; and there was a letter from his own lawyer, who advised him to hurry up and sell his bonds before a new drop in the market which was anticipated. Then there were a few advertisements, and finally there was an anonymous—it turned out—letter from a man who in a rather illegible handwriting instructed Bendix that pornography did not belong in a crime novel. By way of experiment, Bendix had inserted a few erotic scenes in his last novel and himself felt that they were something of a break in the style. At the same time, he felt that the crime novel must somehow keep up with the times. Straus had inserted very realistic erotic scenes in his novels from the beginning; perhaps that was one reason that most of the critics took him more seriously—he had even been the subject of a detailed critical analysis

13

in the literary journal *Vindrosen,* which had also perceived socialistic motifs in Straus' novels.

Bendix read the anonymous letter twice and then threw it in the wastebasket. It was not yet time to do the revision of yesterday's work, but the mail and especially the thought of Straus—who now certainly also sat writing his fall novel, if he wouldn't surprise everybody by putting out a novel for the spring and another for the fall as he had last year—had knocked Bendix off course, and after eating a little lunch, he worked the frozen garden door open and took a walk in the hard-crusted snow. He walked down to the larch tree and ran his fingers over the small firm buds which in three months would become green needles.

Shall we put aside the work until tomorrow? It has been too warm to write, and I must confess that the one thin whiskey has become three. Bendix' beautiful principle of completing a chapter a day is not practical in this climate. And here I sit feeling very strangely satisfied at writing about the Danish winter wearing a pair of sunglasses that tease me by sliding down my nose because it is wet with the same sweat that has drenched the legs in my shorts. During the siesta hour the last wind subsided, and the mosquitoes began to swarm under my umbrella. We should like to get on to this murder, but it will not be today and certainly not tomorrow either. I'll stop now. The garden in snow. The short walk down to the larch tree—oh, imagine being able to work open a magic door and go out into the Danish snow. Oh, imagine being able to walk down to the end of the yard and stand awhile under a Danish larch tree. The cold makes my eyes water, my room-warm glasses steam up, and a fan of white fog pours out of my mouth when I breathe deeply and exhale. I'll switch off the typewriter before I become sentimental. I'll go in for my overdue siesta, and before I fall asleep (if I do fall asleep) I'll think about whether I've chosen the best of all places for writing my Danish winter novel, my ninth (fifth winter novel), which right now I don't feel very certain will ever be finished.

Must approach that murder in an entirely different tempo tomorrow.

February Twelfth

Used the afternoon yesterday to go into the city (bus in, taxi home) and to make several more or less urgent purchases. Bought a coffee percolator of local manufacture so now I no longer need to write on whiskey and a heavy head and a lack of siesta sleep. The coffee, to be sure, doesn't taste like Danish coffee, but that would be asking too much anyway. My most expensive purchase was a very good transistor radio, made by Braun, which is supposed to be able to pick up all the wave lengths you could possibly think of. Managed to get an hour to go by just in reading the directions, used up quite a bit of the evening making coffee in my new percolator (contrary to all my principles about not drinking coffee in the evening, as if I didn't have a hard enough time falling asleep), and tried out the new radio. Naturally my idea was to pick up Denmark on one of the more exotic wave lengths, but I didn't succeed. Still, I did suddenly receive an unexpected jab of homesickness right in the solar plexus: all of a sudden they played something extremely familiar on a distant wave length, and it didn't take me long to place it. For a moment it was only something to do with Copenhagen and my childhood; then it was the romantic composer Lumbye, of course, and in the next moment it was the "Amelie Waltz," and I could still remember a bit of the text from the old Lumbye film (wasn't it called *The Champagne Gallop?*) where they sang to the waltz: "Or was it only a honey heart / that you gave to me?" I thought at first, of course, that I had got a Danish station and that all the money was well spent, but it turned out that Lumbye was being broadcast on a station which, although it perhaps wasn't exactly local, had announcements in a language I guessed belonged to the local language group, and so wasn't very far away. After Lumbye they played Strauss—Strauss with two s's.

At the only newsstand in the city, I tried to get Danish newspapers, but they didn't know a thing about them, not even about the *Politiken*

Weekly, nor any Swedish or Norwegian papers. Therefore I've made sure that in the future I'll get the *Herald Tribune* at breakfast instead of the local paper. But of course I don't expect to get news from home from that quarter.

I have taken my radio out on the veranda, and it plays (interrupted by something that sounds like advertisements) bossa nova and samba and such things. Soft and soothing and good to write to. At the radio shop I momentarily considered buying a stereo set so that I could write to music of my choice as at home, but that would be too complicated and expensive. I don't have, after all, unlimited resources —first I would have to build up a record collection, and the selection here didn't appear too good. Besides, it's not a great idea to play stereophonic music out in the open air, and I'm not about to sit inside just to get my music to work by from two sides.

I promised myself yesterday to get to the murder quickly, and get to it I shall, but I think I must hold off for today and get certain ideas clarified. It's not my usual method, but my ninth novel will not be one of my usual novels. I have to face the fact that I'm starting with a less definite plan than before. It all has to do with several things I don't need to go into right now, but it also has to do with certain things I simply cannot envision. Fortunately, I've made the man a crime writer like myself, and that's a great help. Some people will call it a temporary expedient, but I must try to stop thinking about my critics all the time. When all is said and done, it's quite unlikely that the book will ever be published. Yes, that's my immediate feeling today. I'm writing just to pass the time.

So I'll install the man in my own house. Exit Hellerup, replaced by Nærum. Why must I insist on knowing what the man's house looks like? I'll only have use for it in my first chapter. Nevertheless, I have to—it's just the way I work. So he lives in a corner apartment of a row house in Nærum, 98 yd², with a larch tree at the end of the little yard, and I know precisely how the different rooms are situated in relation to each other. Much of what I wrote yesterday has to be revised, but perhaps the most important thing of all is to get Hellerup revised to Nærum. Or take it out altogether—I don't need to tell the reader where the man lives, but having first written Hellerup, I'm on the wrong track and then there is no longer any larch tree at the end of the yard, either.

I turn off my new radio because I want to keep the "Amelie Waltz" in my mind for a little while. It reminds me of something that will be of use to me if I'm to complete the work I've begun. What is it that it reminds me of? Copenhagen and the end-of-the-season dances. Wartime, train to Østerport, trolley to the Odd Fellows Hall. A sinking feeling in my stomach and examination jitters that aren't lessened by the fact that, after all, it's supposed to be a festive occasion. Actually the lancies minuet was the worst trial, not the waltz— that complicated pattern you were always supposed to keep your place in if you weren't going to ruin it for both yourself and others. I never learned the dance, but there were always helpful hands that reached out to me when I barged off in the wrong direction; there was always someone who hauled me back into the right place at the last moment. Strange that the others could figure it out and I couldn't— I wasn't stupid, after all. Or was I? No, but I let myself get scared. As a matter of fact, I used it later in a novel; I used the lancies as an image of the pattern that a good crime novel follows. Couples and places are exchanged, but one ends up where one began. Strange that I hated that dance, I who love systems and patterns. Right now I'd give a great deal to hear the silly little melodies again.

But I heard Lumbye's "Amelie Waltz" and suddenly it was cold wet Danish spring weather and I stood with my parents in blacked-out Bredgade or—more likely, perhaps—it was afternoon because there must have been a curfew and we had to go to the end-of-the-season dance and I'd been too nervous to eat anything all day and now they would see how much I had learned during the year and in a way the waltz was one of the easiest only you got so breathless from it. I've stopped using commas; it is a trick that can be used in moderation. Write breathlessly about a breathless memory.

Why do I write so much about examinations? I've generally done well in them, after all. Things have gone fine with me; I became an author who could live by his writing. But that's not what I should be writing about today, when I have to break my promise and scarcely get any further toward the murder that Bang ends his day by committing. (Yes, I have changed the name. Bendix is completely impossible in the genitive, and there is something to be said for single-syllabled names when you expect to use them thousands of times in the course of the book. Think of having to write Højberg-Pedersen every time you refer to him.) I'm still putting off the difficult work a little, but names fascinate me. On that ground alone, being a writer is a desirable job: you get lots of children to baptize. Why Bang, then? Hopefully there won't be anyone who takes it symbolically: Bang, you're dead. Anyway, it is of course rather onomatopoetic, and it is very ordinary too. Onomatopoetic, but not symbolic. Straus loves names that *mean* something or other, preferably two things at once. The same with titles. He could come up with the idea of calling a book something like *Chain* and make a big thing out of its meaning two completely opposite things. Partly that you had past ties, partly that these were a burden. I talk about Straus in my new book. Try to find several titles that have more than one meaning. Straus could come up with the idea of calling a thick black book *Testament* in fine gold lettering. An idea to consider. Back to the business of names: some sort of taboo simply forbids me to name characters Hansen or Jensen.

The assignment for the day is to move Bang into my own house. The corner apartment in a row house in Nærum, view over the marsh behind the 400 yd² yard. Between the yard and the marsh is Rundforbivej Road, everything covered with Danish snow. As usual, I have to know much more than I use. The house is set on a hillside and, like my own, is a split-level—three steps down from the dining room to the living room, three steps down from the hallway to the bedroom. The study is adjacent to the living room and both have the same view: the windows face west. Then there are the entryway, the kitchen, the utility room, and the guest room. I'll undoubtedly have much more difficulty with how Straus lives, but I'll worry about that when the time comes. Then there is Nadja's apartment. No, I must solve the problems gradually as they present themselves—right now the important thing is to get a grip on Chapter One.

Bang's house shows evidence of the fact that until a few months ago two people lived in it and now there is only one. There is furniture missing, and there are light spots on the walls where pictures have been taken down and large gaps in the bookcases because of the books she has taken with her. In the kitchen, suddenly very elementary things are lacking, such as a bottle opener or a toaster. The bed is still made up for two. Bang isn't used to sleeping alone in it, and that has made his normal difficulty in sleeping (which I can use) even greater. The telephone rings less frequently and there is less mail. The laundry basket in the utility room still holds the scent of Nadja's perfume, La Chamade. A reviewer once wrote that I was auditive (good dialogue), visual (four of my novels have been made into movies, one of them by a Swedish company), and what's it called when you are smell-oriented, because he thought I was that too; but he concluded by complaining that I was not at all tactile. Now, admittedly I have written that you can't teach an old dog new tricks, but I'm not that old after all, and wouldn't it be a good idea to resolve to make my new novel infernally *tactile?* I can at least make an attempt. Try to write tactually about Nadja instead of smearing her all over with scents.

On the whole, Nadja is the problem. Nadja and Straus, but first Nadja. One of these days I'll sit down and just write about her without thinking of whether or not it can be used in the novel. Of course, I'll use my eyes, and I'll try to find a style of dialogue for her, and I'll sniff her as I usually sniff all my girls, but I'll also touch her—I'll create a little étude in tactile description of women. And not only Nadja; the whole book (still need a title) will be very *tactile.* Then you can be sure that not a single reviewer will notice.

Resolution of the day: Not another word about reviewers. How did I once put it in an interview? I write for myself. If I amuse myself (yes, amuse myself) writing a book, I naïvely assume that there will be some who will amuse themselves reading it. Used the word *amuse* with cool deliberation in order to be sure not to give the impression that I took myself seriously. Writing as a profession and not as a calling. But now: Not another word about critics today. I still have an hour before it gets too hot to write, and I'll use it for a few (hopefully very *tactile*) notes about Nadja—so I'll feel I know her a little better before I write further in the novel (I'd like to continue with it in the morning).

How I admire authors who write from their imagination and never require living models. Straus . . . but I've promised myself to ration Straus a little. In my own writing I'm dependent on what I have experienced, and even if I blend my experiences very skillfully, I have the feeling that I am recognizable in what I write, and I'm afraid that people I know will feel I'm stepping on their toes. The Spy, they call me—it has gradually become a cliché that the small-town reviewers have adopted. Now, to bolster myself up a bit, I'll construct a scene between Bang and Nadja (that's how it is, you get on a first-name basis with girls) and then I'll probably step on the toes of she-herself-knows-whom. Or will she be a little flattered? The thought that she'll never get to read it—partly because it won't be included in the book, partly because right now I can't imagine how the book could be published—reassures me a little. Perhaps it will also help me to write a little more freely.

Bang comes home from the city. What has he done in the city, this writer who works at home? Oh, yes, he has recorded a drama review at the radio station, and he has visited the newspaper *Politiken* to talk with Mogensen about an article, or he has been at Gyldendal Publishers and announced his upcoming project for Mogens Knudsen, or he has been up at Fromberg's to find out how many copies of his book from last year have sold up to now. They have gone through Bang's whole backlist of sales; with eight books behind him, there is always activity. Bang is an author who works at home, but still he has errands in the city, and now and then he drives in at random for the simple reason that he has had enough of writing and feels the need to see people. He is frequently utilized as a feature writer and a free-lance man in radio. He can be called upon to write about things other than crime, but he keeps his distance from anything approaching politics, and he has, in contrast to Straus—but we'll unquestionably get to that —a very firm rule that he'll never write about his colleagues.

Anyway, Bang comes home late from a trip to the city, so late that Nadja has arrived home (from her job as a script girl at the TV station) before him. She has the car—the car is simply hers; he sees it parked outside the house, but there is no light in the kitchen, though it should be time to make dinner. Moist air greets him in the entryway, and when he hangs his coat in the closet, he notices that the door to the bathroom is open and the light is on in there. She is sitting in the bathtub reading the popular woman's magazine *Eva*. She has not yet begun to wash herself. She is just steeping and both her hands are dry. When she looks up and sees him, she asks him to get a beer for each of them and cigarettes and an ashtray.

Bang comes back to the bathroom and sits down on the toilet after having handed her a beer and put the ashtray on the edge of the tub. The bathtub is too small for Bang. He can't stretch out in it, and the only way he can get his whole body down into the warm water is by assuming a fetus position. It's just about as bad for Nadja. She has filled the tub to the brim; the water comes up to her shoulders, and the surface is covered with green foam, which slowly begins to dissolve so he can see her breasts and knees. He knows that when she begins to use the soap the foam will disappear quickly and he'll be able to see her whole body. After seven years of marriage, he still looks forward to the sight.

He tells her about his day and she tells him about hers. She has pulled her hair back with a rubber band so that it won't get wet. She sweats profusely, although she doesn't use bathwater as hot as Bang does—this ability to sweat easily makes her more comfortable than Bang when traveling in warm countries; Bang can't sweat, but rather holds the heat inside him like a steadily increasing irritant. Her cheeks are red and her ears, which for once are exposed, are very, very red. Sweating and being red become her.

Her cigarette doesn't burn well in the steaming bathroom, and Bang bends over her to light it again. He gets a little wet thank-you kiss, the first of the day. Now one can see deep down into the green bathwater, and he can't resist the temptation to caress her wet neck. She drinks a little of her beer—Bang has only brought a glass for himself, he knows that she prefers to drink from the bottle—and sweats even more. *Eva* now lies on the tile floor curling in the moisture. Then she pulls out the bath plug and lets about half the water drain out so she can wash the upper half of her body. Bang enjoys the sight of her soaping her breasts; her nipples, like everything else about her, are redder than usual. She lets a little more water out and washes her stomach, Bang helping her with her back and trying to make the strokes of the washcloth like soft caresses. Finally she nearly empties the tub and washes between her legs. She lifts her bottom a little and rubs with the washcloth until her hair is covered with a rich soapy foam. Then she does her legs and knees, and finally she takes the plug out, puts on her shower cap so that her dark hair is covered up, and rinses herself with the hand shower. When she steps out of the tub, Bang stands ready with the large ocher-yellow Turkish towel. But instead of beginning to dry her, he presses her to him, and, laughing, she gives up being dried for the moment and instead presses her wet body against him so he himself gets wet. He gets two wet spots on his shirt—he has left his jacket out in the hallway—and two more wet spots where her knees press against his pants legs.

The vapor from her body steams his glasses while he kisses her wet red cheeks. He takes off her shower cap. Her hair is wet and small drops of sweat run down her scalp and over her forehead or down her neck. She sweats long after she has got out of the tub. She usually sits and smokes a cigarette or two before the sweat has stopped enough to make it worthwhile for her to take a fresh bath towel and dry herself again and get dressed. He presses her against the damp bathroom wall, which is so cold that she comes into his arms again and amuses herself by getting his good clothes as wet as she can. As is characteristic of her, she continues smoking while she caresses him with her wet hands. She loosens his tie and unbuttons the top buttons of his shirt. Is it hanging straight down? she asks, and he shakes his head. She throws the cigarette butt into the toilet and pushes him a step backward so he ends up standing on *Eva*. She worms a wet hand in under his waistband and begins to caress him. She never caresses him roughly, and since his pants are so tight that it is hard for her to move her hand gently, she carefully unbuttons them. She is expert at figuring out how to unbutton or unzip his different pants—just as skillful as he is clumsy about figuring out the hooks and buttons and zippers and other mechanics of her clothes. A moment later he stands with his pants and shorts down around his ankles on the wet bathroom floor.

He kisses her on the neck, where she most likes to be kissed, and caresses her body, which is already beginning to dry. He guides a hand up between her legs and moves his fingertips around in the wet curled hair. She presses her stomach forward until his hand is squeezed tight, takes off his glasses and puts them on the edge of the sink, unbuttons his shirt all the way while she whispers: Right now? He nods. I've put something in the oven, she says. He asks if she can't turn the oven down a little, and she nods.

Down in the bedroom she sits on the edge of the bed and perfumes herself. She daubs a touch of Chamade behind her ears, a little on each wrist, a fingertip between her breasts, and another fingertip in her groin. It is an established ritual—he is accustomed to seeing it, and yet he enjoys it. She has a cigarette in the corner of her mouth, and he restrains himself, as countless times before, from asking her not to smoke now—not because he's impatient, but because it seems a bit prosaic to him. He can't see her altogether clearly now because his glasses have been left in the bathroom. Of the two of them, he is unquestionably the more romantic: it's he who doesn't think they should talk now, it's he who doesn't answer when she, while she smokes and perfumes herself, questions him about how he's spent his day in the city. He has turned on the radiator so that she won't get cold, he has closed the drapes, and he has gone into the living room and got a couple of candles because he doesn't like making love in the dark. He can't manage without the stimulation of looking at her while he caresses her and she caresses him.

She takes her time with her cigarette, and finally, unable to control his impatience, he takes it out of her mouth and butts it. She has a bad habit of smoking much too close to the filter anyway. On the night table is a pack of cigarettes for afterward, as well as the little bottle of perfume and the little larger spray perfume and the ashtray. Bang doesn't smoke afterward because he only smokes cigars; besides, he thinks it's too prosaic, although he often would like a large cigar when it's over and he lies there feeling good. It's not very pleasant, either, to have the little bedroom smelling of cigars; they will have to sleep there in a few hours and the room is difficult to air out.

She slowly lies down backward across the width of the bed, and he bends down over her and kisses her between her legs. Have you pulled out the telephone extension? she asks, and again it annoys him that she is thinking so practically now, but then one of them must think practically, and in these situations it is always she. He has an erection, and he realizes that he looks a little comic as he goes over to the window and pulls out the telephone contact. But she isn't looking at him—she has stretched out lengthwise on the bed with her head on the pillow and is waiting for him. He lies down on his side next to her, their hands cross, and they caress each other—she with her gentle hands, he a little more violently because he knows she likes it that way. Paradoxically, of the two, it is always he who wants and needs the longest foreplay.

Her face is clearly visible, but already the candles behind her are out of focus. Her forehead is still slightly wet, especially around her hairline, and her hair is damp and lusterless. He lies there wondering why she generally attracts him most intensely in situations which are mundane and actually shouldn't be particularly flattering. He can be attracted to her when she stands bent over the oven and the whole kitchen is steaming with food preparation. There is something about moisture which becomes her. He likes to travel with her in warm countries; it doesn't bother him that her hair hangs limply, nor does it bother him that her sweat dampens the edge of her collar or her sleeves, or that it seeps through the armpits of her dress. He often feels like photographing her when she is sweating or when she is still steamy after a bath, but he has never got permission to do that. She has always wanted to appear at her best when he takes pictures of her, and he has never been allowed to photograph her with curlers in her hair or with her face covered with cleansing cream. On the whole, she doesn't very much like to be photographed—he wants to have time to get the proper focus and to compose the picture so it won't be necessary to crop it afterward, but she doesn't have the patience for that and may decide to light a cigarette while he stands there reading the light meter and getting the correct focus. That's why he has many pictures in which she is smoking—which doesn't really matter because she looks like herself as he has come to love her when she has a cigarette dangling from the corner of her mouth and is squinting one eye a little because of the smoke.

He caresses her neck and shoulders with his left hand the way she likes it done, while his right hand presses firmly against her groin and his index finger and middle finger alternately penetrate her. She is very wet, and it's not only his finger that gets sticky—the moisture seeps out of her until her entire groin is wet and he has the feeling that her moisture is dripping onto the sheet as well. Suddenly she stops caressing him, settles back passively a moment with her legs spread a little more apart, and he moves forward over her and glides into her. He doesn't want anything to happen for a moment and lies there purposely thinking about something else entirely. When he wants to pull himself out, she squeezes together as if she could hold on to him, and he can't free himself from the thought that in a way it's all something that she just wants to get over and done with. It's always that way between them; it's always she who is urgent, and the thought crosses his mind that there must be something he does wrong—perhaps only some little thing or other—for it should be the other way around, after all. But maybe she's only thinking that she has put something in the oven and there's a limit to how long it can stay there without spoiling.

Actually, he likes the feeling of her squeezing—it seems like a little caress, although it isn't meant that way; it's just a signal. And he takes note of the signal. The next time he goes into her he stays there, and together they find the right rhythm, and suddenly she lets go of him and grips the bedposts behind her with both hands and presses her heels into the mattress while her breathing shifts from her mouth, which she presses closed, to her nose, which is next to his right ear, and a moment later he comes himself, and he tries to keep thrusting even though he is nearly out of commission in order to get it to last longer, but he is finished nevertheless and already begins to get small while she is gasping for breath and expelling two streams of warm air from her nostrils right against his cheek.

Afterward she sits hunched over in bed smoking, while he draws on her back with a cautious finger. What did I draw? he asks. A cat, she replies, because he always draws a cat. No, he says, today it was a dog. It was a cat, she replies. Don't you think I know your cats? She smokes the cigarette right down to the filter and then walks naked out to the kitchen to check on dinner. He hears her bare feet in the hallway, and he hears the water running in the bathroom. He can feel that if she came back now he would be able to once more, but she is putting her clothes on. The little Japanese radio alarm clock, which wakens one with music in the mornings, says seven, and he swings his legs out of bed. He is beginning to feel hungry. A slight despondency is quickly brushed aside—it has been a good day, his new book is selling well, and there is a steady sale of the books on his backlist. He gets finished in the bathroom quickly, and afterward helps Nadja set the table. Out in the kitchen he fondles Nadja, delaying her systematically in her work until she nudges him gently away with her bottom. He carries the candles from the bedroom to the table, lights a small stick of incense to please her, and opens a bottle of red wine because it seems like a day to celebrate. They toast one another, and her eyes have a special luster that tells him she is feeling good right now. He is very much in love with her—he is as happy as he can be.

Nadja. I want to make Nadja very alive before I kill her.

February Thirteenth

Bang turned and looked up toward the house. There were no footprints in the snow other than his own, which led from the garden door down toward the spot where he was now standing under the larch tree. It was one o'clock. For an hour or two it would still be light enough to see the blue color of the window frames which he himself had painted that first summer they had had the house together. None of the other houses had window frames painted in a bright color; the clear Corbusier blue had been Nadja's choice, and she had helped him with the work.

Through the large living-room window he could see the bare wall over the sofa where one of her pictures had hung, and he suddenly felt like doing something to fill up the empty room a little. He broke off a few large branches from the larch tree and carried them up to the house, following his own tracks in the snow. Would they bud in the warm room? It was worth a try.

He put them in a yellow vase by the window where they would get the best light and then began reading through the previous day's chapter, but after a few pages he couldn't go any further. It wasn't bad, but still it wasn't right. Did he really know this traveling salesman that the whole thing was about? Did he really know the little country town where most of the action would take place? One of Bang's friends had earned money for school one summer as a traveling book salesman, and Bang had invited him home one evening for red wine, cheese, and cross-examination. The books were a help in the cross-examination—books were something Bang knew a lot about and could sink his teeth into. For the country town he had used as his model the only one he knew, the one in which he had spent his summer vacations during the Occupation. He knew its geography and something of its atmosphere, but he didn't know, for example, its night life and its gossip—and the Occupation was twenty-five years ago. Good, then he had to use his imagination; he had to invent what he didn't know. It was about time—it was a challenge. What he had written wasn't bad either, but there was something wrong with it, and he suddenly gave up reading any further in it and went to the telephone instead. He had remembered something that must have been nagging his subconscious for days. It was the twenty-sixth of January and there were only five days left to fill out his tax form; since the beginning of the month all he had done was to lay his numerous earnings statements in a little stack next to the stack of bills.

He telephoned his accountant, but the number was busy—others were undoubtedly in the same situation he was. After a few unsuccessful attempts to get through, he asked the operator to complete the call and then cleared away the mess from breakfast and lunch and his morning's work. After half an hour his call came through. During that half-hour when he felt he couldn't leave the house, he had begun to feel uncomfortable in the empty rooms. He had felt a greater and greater urge to break out, to leave the house, to go to the city and look up someone he could talk with. The accountant, after consulting his appointment book, gave him an appointment for that evening. Next year you might call me a little earlier, he said pleasantly before he hung up.

Bang put on his fur coat and went out to the car. On the way into the city he made plans. He had to do something to get out of his depressed state, and the best thing would be to contact some of the people who were figures of stability for him in his work. He parked in front of Østifterne's Credit Bureau and walked over to the Politiken Building. Opposite the Troelstrup Department Store he realized he had forgotten to put any money in the parking meter out of sheer joy at having found a parking place, but now he had gone too far to turn back, and it usually didn't matter anyway. He went up to Mogensen's office, knocked on the door, and got the usual slightly delayed but cheerful come in.

He hadn't thought ahead of time about what he wanted to say and had to improvise. He explained that he was in the middle of a novel and for that reason had been out of touch for some time, but now he felt like writing a feature article and wanted to hear what Mogensen thought about the subject. There is certainly a trend toward (here the telephone rang—someone on the other end was so upset that it could be heard clearly in the office, and Mogensen's angelic patient explanation that the person's feature article had not been dropped but just delayed because of more pressing material gave Bang a better chance to think through what he wanted to suggest). There is certainly a trend toward, he began again when Mogensen at last had said goodbye to the troublesome feature writer, taking the crime novel more and more seriously. Bang himself had done this in his article "Forced into a Corner," but now he wanted to do something else. He wanted to write about the crime novel's future and raise the question of whether one doesn't risk taking the life—that is, the spontaneity—out of it by analyzing it too thoroughly and regarding it as a social and psychological and moral and every other kind of document. Wasn't there a risk that all these analyses made crime writers too self-conscious and reflective? Hadn't jazz in its time been made into a bloodless "highbrow" culture purely because of analysis and self-analysis? Wasn't the same thing about to happen with beat music? Bang warmed to his subject and even improvised a title: "Bloodless Murder."

The telephone rang again. After Mogensen had handled another impatient feature writer with velvet gloves, he lit his pipe and glanced once at his watch while Bang tried to pick up the thread of their conversation and discovered that he had already talked too long about an article which was not even written yet. I'd like to hear if it sounds to you like an idea worth developing, he concluded.

Mogensen hesitated a moment. Basically, yes, he replied, but I can't promise to publish it right away. As you yourself heard, there's a lot of pressure, and then, as it happened, Straus dropped by this morning, and he's also writing about the future of the crime novel. His article is right here. I haven't had time to read it yet. Curiously enough, he calls it just that, "The Future of the Crime Novel." Well, anyway, he came first, so . . . (Mogensen straightened a little pile of manuscripts in front of him) . . . so if his article is all right, and I'm sure it will be, then we'll certainly have to wait a month at least with yours. I'm planning to publish Straus on Sunday, so you can read it then and see if it doesn't inspire you. I don't think you two are in agreement because, as far as I understand him, his contention is precisely that the crime novel must become conscious of its social function. This is, of course, a point that was made when they wrote about him in *Vindrosen,* too. As far as I know, it's the first time *Vindrosen* has taken the crime novel seriously, so one would have to say that Straus has done something for the genre even if you think there's a risk of the crime novel becoming too . . . In principle, I don't completely disagree with you that there is a danger, perhaps especially as far as . . . the . . . lesser lights. Yes, but read Straus on Sunday and see if he doesn't inspire you. Anyway, you can figure on about a month. . . .

Bang leaned back a little in the visitor's chair where Straus had been sitting a few hours ago. The desire to write a feature article had vanished as quickly as it had sprung up. He didn't want to write an article which would appear to be just an answer to something Straus had written. Mogensen hadn't read Straus' article yet; still he obviously had decided to publish it in the Sunday edition. Other writers hounded the editors and applied all sorts of pressure, and Straus could just go into the city, lay a manuscript in front of Mogensen, and be assured that it would be published the next Sunday, as fast as it could possibly be type-set, proofread, and printed. And then Bang would be allowed to read Straus' article and "answer" it in a month, or allow himself to be inspired by it. But Bang's article would not be published in the Sunday edition—at least, his articles never had been.

Listen, I have to be running along, Mogensen said and got up. Bang got up too, said goodbye, and walked toward the door. Instead of accompanying him, Mogensen sat down again. His little maneuver of standing up had obviously been only a symbolic expression of how busy he was. As a last polite gesture or as a means of getting the conversation going again, Bang wanted to say something in the doorway about the Poe Club; he wanted to ask if there was going to be another meeting soon, but the telephone on Mogensen's desk started ringing, and Bang closed the door carefully behind him and walked down to the Raadhusplads.

So Straus was in the city. Straus had come in from his South Zealand country estate, which Bang had seen only in illustrated reports in magazines, and with his usual incomprehensible sense of timing, he had managed to lay a manuscript about the crime novel's future on Mogensen's desk a few hours before Bang himself arrived. Straus was in the city, and Straus didn't come into the city just to deliver a manuscript to Mogensen, a manuscript he could have got published in the Sunday paper without a personal visit. Straus must have had other errands.

It was getting dark in the Raadhusplads—the asphalt sparkled with frost and the neon thermometer on the Rich Building, which shouldn't be called the Rich Building any more now that the Rich ersatz coffee advertising on it had been replaced by an advertisement for Irma Coffee (does anyone at all use ersatz coffee any more? yes, in Bang's new novel, in the little country town—that was a good idea, a good detail), read fourteen degrees Fahrenheit. Bang stood there for a while looking out over the square and taking deep breaths of the cold air. Then he turned and began to study the display of Danish books in the Politiken Bookstore window. In the center of the display window was a little pile of *Stay out of Sight* and on the top of the pile a single copy of the book was propped upright with a marker stuck into it. The marker had a picture of Straus' face and under it a quotation from a well-known Norwegian critic: "Kept me awake all day and all night too . . . he should have been born in Norway."— Johan Borgen. Bang looked for his own novel published the previous fall and found it a little farther back in the window. Gyldendal had made a special marker for his book too, but it wasn't used here. Unlike Straus, whose first name was no longer used in publicity about him, the publicity for Bang used both his names. We wouldn't want you confused with Herman Bang, would we now? someone had said— most likely Mogens Knudsen—when Bang suggested he should be on a last-name-only basis with his readers too. Generally the little word Straus set across the top of the book jacket in gaudy grotesque took up more room than the title of the book. Straus had become a trademark, while Anthon Bang remained an explanation of who had written this particular book. But it would have looked splendid: an enormous BANG, two letters shorter than Straus and so the letters could be even bigger, but there was no hope for that, it seemed.

You did have to say, though, that Bang's books were invariably more attractive than Straus'. They were perhaps less eye-catching, but they had better over-all craftsmanship. That was because Straus simply turned in his manuscripts and left the rest to the publisher, whereas Bang painstakingly followed his books along their way, came up with suggestions for the design, and held long conferences with the art department and involved himself all the way through the struggle of producing his book jackets. The results were quite satisfying. Sooner or later, due to the time schedule, compromises had to be made. But Bang was well aware that a certain elementary effectiveness was often lacking in his cunning ideas, an effectiveness which was further weakened by tasteful and meticulous graphic presentation. *In the Same Boat* was a more handsome book than *Stay out of Sight,* but it simply didn't resemble a crime novel, and now, half a year later, Bang well understood why his publishers hadn't been particularly enthusiastic about the title. After their first books, both Bang and Straus had got away from using words like "murder" and "corpse" in their titles, but Straus was more gifted at making a title sound threatening anyway. It wasn't only the alliteration that made *Stay out of Sight* a better title, but also all that threatening play upon the lonely children's game which adults should have put behind them, but which they can't shake off. *In the Same Boat* was a good title too—it was appropriate insofar as it covered the relationship between the psychopath and the nice guy bound helplessly to one another, thanks to the secret they share (and to the fact that they begin to resemble each other more and more), but there wasn't a real threat in the title unless you had already read the book, and it wasn't pithy and idiomatic, although it didn't have many more syllables than Straus' title.

On the way to his car Bang thought about the title for his next book. At first he thought about calling it *The Wrong Man,* but there was a film called that. Then he thought about *The Bedeviled Man,* which had the advantage of meaning two things: the police had got hold of the wrong man (bedeviling him), and under the pressure of suspicion the man is well on his way to becoming crazy (bedeviled). But Panduro had written a novel called *The Bedeviled Man,* so that wouldn't do, either. Bang provisionally considered *No One Knows the Day,* and that was also a good title (a bit of the threatening quality that Straus was so good with), but the title had the disadvantage of reminding one more of Branner's *No One Knows the Night* than of Ingemann's hymn: "Blessed, blessed, each soul that has peace! Still no one knows the day before the sun goes down." It was threatening, and it had connections back to childhood, but what good was that when everyone Bang told the title to was reminded of Branner instead of Ingemann?

He had got the little melody into his head now, and it stayed there. Probably it had not been Weyse who wrote the melody, which is in all its conciseness too intellectual, but which grabs hold of you so you can't get rid of it again. The words grab hold of you, too, for that matter—they are so simple and naïve, and then suddenly there is that little snap with *still.* "Still no one knows the day before the sun goes down." Just think if he had written *but.* That would have been good too, but slacker. The little *still* was like an elastic that sent the whole rest of the line into place with a snap.

Humming, Bang got behind the wheel of his car, and it was only then that he noticed the yellow ticket stuck under the windshield wiper. He let it stay there, and when he had driven a little way it flew off. There was always the chance that they had copied down his number incorrectly or would let the matter drop—in any case, that was what had happened to him a couple of times before. Still humming, and with Ingemann's words still running through his mind, he drove down toward Farimag Street and then ventured into the center of the city in order to find a parking place as close as possible to Gyldendal in Klareboderne Street. "Blessed, blessed, each soul that has peace!" ran through his head while he steered the wide car through increasingly narrower streets. "Still no one (that *still* was really good) knows the day before the sun goes down."

And here we leave Bang for today. My hands are shaking a little because I've smoked too much and have drunk too much coffee, which is perhaps no healthier than writing on whiskey. Haven't I got quite a bit done these three days? The characters have been introduced, and even though I haven't kept my resolution to get to the murder in a hurry, all the same I think you must be able to sense that something or other is about to happen, and that's the most important thing. The only thing troubling me and which, along with the overdose of coffee and Henry Clay cigars, will probably keep me awake all during siesta time is that there isn't any possibility of looking up the hymn. It's really not so very long since I looked at it, but now suddenly I'm not so sure. Am I praising Ingemann for my own ingenious idea? Does his hymn really say *but* and not *still?*

Oh, to have a Danish hymnbook to banish the sleepless midday hours. I'd like to read all of Ingemann's hymns and learn them by heart again, as I knew them in my childhood.

February Fifteenth

Why have I skipped a day?

Because I drank myself into a stupor yesterday, as one should be allowed to do once in a while.

How am I today?

Three guesses.

Then why am I writing anyway?

To keep my fingers nimble. It's late afternoon and my hangover is easing up. The world's thinnest whiskey stands on my table with its two icecubes clinking against each other from the slight vibration of the typewriter's motor (if my language is somewhat less than perfect today, there is a reason for it). The sun is poised right between the two palm trees I can see from my veranda, and it no longer burns the skin. It's no longer little and white—it's turned yellow, and in a little while it will turn red and at the same time become steadily larger until it tumbles into the water, and then darkness will come so quickly that I'll have to move indoors immediately in order to see what I'm writing. But perhaps I don't need to see what I'm writing. Right now I just want to keep writing away—it makes me feel calmer.

Why did I drink yesterday?

A conspiracy of circumstances, the way it is when things go wrong. First a sleepless night with an endless repetition of all of Ingemann's morning and evening songs. Mysterious weather with flashes of lightning before it got light. Then suddenly the lights in the room went out and the power was off until lunchtime. By that time I had got the porter to bring me a fresh bottle of bourbon and, a little later, a bottle of sleeping pills—called Vitanil, by God. Hardly a replacement for my good old Noludar, and the effect combined with alcohol was really strange. I became wide awake and plagued by intense physical restlessness. Wanted some coffee, which the power failure made impossible (I'm well aware that my sentences can't stand close grammatical scrutiny today). Got a headache in the middle of everything and had local headache pills delivered too—here you obviously don't need a prescription for anything whatsoever; on the other hand, the pills don't work, or their effect is just the opposite of what you want. All in all, during the course of the night and the morning I mixed a bottle of bourbon with two Vitanils and two Codytranquils, whereupon I found myself in a never-before-experienced condition of wakefulness, giddiness, headache, tiredness, and drunkenness. Next the traditional blackout, which was different from its predecessors only in duration: eighteen hours if I figure correctly, but very likely I don't. Did I answer my question? Not really, I guess, but after all I can ask it again in a little while.

Why am I suffering from sleeplessness now?

Because I have begun to write. That immediately makes it sound as if writing is a "calling" or a "martyrdom," but I'm just telling the truth—I pay for my pleasure with my night's sleep. It's an occupational disease, just like my rheumatism. How do I avoid making myself interesting? How do I damn up (mixed metaphor) this fog of self-pity and self-seriousness which—I can't finish this sentence, but the most important thing is that I know what I mean even though I can't put it into words. How? Christ, after all, the man writes crime novels. Certainly the most honest thing to do would be to stand up on a chair and shout that one *is* interesting, God damn it! Rather than this false modesty—I'm thinking of my own little "pleasure." And, to be completely honest, I must also add that it is a pleasure nevertheless. I think I'll have Straus say in an interview that "it's simply *fun* to write." The fact is that, whichever attitude one chooses, it becomes false, and therefore one shouldn't talk shop at all—but that's also an attitude, and so one might just as well blabber on. On to the next question, which is:

Why do I use the question-and-answer method today?

Because I want to be kind to myself today, and this method is easy. I don't require the great (!) overview and keep myself occupied anyway. I've swiped the idea from (hurry up: *sans comparaison*) (I can't spell in French) Joyce (the insignificant crime writer compares himself —no, no more of that). But back to the case at hand: a lot of questions have turned up, and if I am to sleep tonight (I've dumped the bottle of Vitanils into the sink—I don't dare take them) I'll have to try to get a few of them answered.

What should the novel be called?

Yes, *there* I'm in the fortunate position of being able to choose. I can use one of Bang's titles and actually I can also use one of Straus' titles —both make sense. In some mysterious way or other, all the titles I can think of for this book are suitable, and that should perhaps be taken as a sign that there is something fundamentally wrong some place, but I don't take it as such, at least not today. I could also call the book *No One Knows the Day,* but I've already let Bang reflect on what is wrong with that title. Too similar to Branner. I can't use *The Bedeviled Man* either—Panduro beat me to it; otherwise it would have been fine. *In the Same Boat* is—for reasons which will become apparent later—also an amazingly appropriate (I don't know what's the matter with my writing today) title and I'll consider it, but it's true, as they said at Gyldendal—I'll get to that tomorrow, God willing —there isn't much punch to it. Perhaps we should go back to the old style and include a little "murder" in the title. *It Began with Murder.* Could be used only if I can jazz things up right in the beginning of the book. "It began with murder and . . ." Well, I don't know, I'm not wild about the dot-dot-dot style. I'll let the problem rest safely in my subconscious, which will certainly come up with more suggestions —it isn't that which keeps me awake. More a slight suspiciousness at the fact that there are so many titles which are appropriate. Should no doubt worry about it, so I'll soon think of a new question.

What was Bang's first novel called?

One or Two Murders. That was before he acquired refined sensibilities.

What was Straus' first novel called?

Murder, Maybe, until I think of something better. In any case, it has to be something with alliteration.

More titles from the gentlemen?

Not right now—I've run dry.

O.K. What does Bang look like?

Let me answer with a counter-question. How much does the reader enjoy getting a description of the man? That he is tall and fair or short and dark? Not a great deal, I'd say. Maybe it actually obstructs the imagination—the reader's, that is. There should be some room for his own invention, for putting something of himself into the main character. It should be possible for the main character to be anyone at all. Simenon quotes in an interview some great literary light or other: Who can be the main character in a novel? Answer: Anyone at all, driven to the extreme. Another thing is that, as a rule, the novel's point of view is that of the main character. He can see the others; he can't see himself. Unless the author puts him in front of a mirror, which I did myself in the first chapter of my first novel.

What does Nadja look like?

Today I'm most in favor of black hair. Under the influence of a dream or a memory, have chosen to change the model as far as outward appearance is concerned. In order to fool the enemy, which I need to strive harder for on the whole. Black hair with brown squirrel eyes or greenish brown. The first wrinkles under her eyes, and fillings at the base of her back teeth when she smiles. She looks used—a reminder that she is usable. She generally wears black or dark-colored clothes. Her skin is warm, she never gets cold, she can easily begin to smell a little of sweat; not old sweat but new "clean" sweat, an attractive warm smell. But now I'm sniffing around again and quite a distance from the question.

Straus?

While I think of it, Straus' first book could be called *Murder in Waltztime*. Admittedly, the alliteration is missing, but, on the other hand, it points up the author's self-centeredness: he knows very well what people will think of when they hear his name. That was in the beginning—later his name becomes a trademark, and there is no longer anyone who thinks of the king of the waltz when they see Straus' books in the store windows. Perhaps *Run Wild in Waltztime?* No, that isn't really Straus. Well, what does he look like? If you could explain to the reader that he resembles the French actor Philippe Noiret, it would save a lot of trouble, but you can't do that because readers don't know what Philippe Noiret looks like. But he does— that I've decided, that I know. A large calm face with a pair of lively eyes. Perhaps not so much lively as alive. A man who drinks and eats so well it comes as a bit of a surprise when you realize that he is present in those eyes all the time. That he spies, too. He is better at it than Bang—not so obvious. He wears good clothing—he goes in for the landed-gentry style: heavy tweed, comfortable clothes with a slightly sporty touch which calls to mind the fact that he goes hunting with his wife. A few years ago he experimented with various lengths of hair and beard; now he has settled on one image; and yet there is enough life in his eyes so no one makes the mistake of thinking Straus *really* sticks to a single role. He can still play the street urchin, and his heavy body can come to life when he realizes that the TV camera is focused on him. Something like that—I'm still trying to zero in on the target as far as Straus is concerned, but it doesn't matter that I don't see him clearly yet because for the time being his role is to be invisibly present.

Why the absurd name?

An inspired impulse, which has clung to me and has grown into an obsession. The combination of something musical and something that rips, rolls, scratches, scrapes, everything possible with an "r" in it. The internationality of the name, its sense of an entity, "a Straus," "my Straus," etc. I may still get around to changing Bang and Nadja, but Straus I won't touch.

What's all this about Straus living on a country estate?

A few years ago he married an honest-to-goodness countess. Although it was a quiet wedding, it attracted a great deal of attention. They have separate holdings, but Straus is good for more than she is.

Straus goes hunting. What does Bang do when he's not writing crime novels?

Tries to translate Nabokov's *Pale Fire* (a tip for the critics)!

Why are you writing about Bang?

To get rid of Bang?

Why are you writing about Straus?

To get rid of Straus!

What's the book about?

Jealousy.

Why are you sitting here?

February Sixteenth

After maneuvering the car around the same block several times, Bang
gave up and parked in an embassy parking place. On his way over to
the publishing house he contemplated what his errand really was. It
depended a little on whom he could get to talk to. It was after four
o'clock and in all probability most of them had left.

You might just as well begin at the top, he thought when he stood
in the reception room, and luck was with him, for Mogens Knudsen
was just about to leave, but he hadn't gone yet. Bang was invited in,
and Knudsen laid his coat, which he'd been about to put on, on the
table.

—Have a chair. It appears to be crime writers' day today. Straus
was just here.

Bang sat down and was offered a cigar. While he clipped it and lit
it, he sat thinking about Straus sitting in the same chair, probably with
an identical cigar, perhaps a few minutes ago. If Bang hadn't wasted
so much time parking, they might have bumped into each other at the
entrance or even in the reception room. Straus had taken the same
route through the city today as Bang—he was always just a little bit
ahead. Where was he now? Bang didn't know himself what the next
stop on his own route would be, but he did know how he would react
if he were told one more time that Straus, by the way, had just gone
out the door.

—It's nice to see you. Are you working on something for us?
Mogens Knudsen asked. The book you talked about last time—have
you begun it?

Bang couldn't remember that he had already talked about his
project. That made his visit even more superfluous.

—A glass of sherry?

While the sherry was being poured, Bang tried to think whether
there wasn't something he could tell about or suggest. He wanted to

hear what the final figures for the Christmas sales were, but he didn't think he could start right in with that.

—You wanted to write about a man accused of a crime he hasn't committed and who has to take the case into his own hands, as far as I can remember. Is that still it?

—Yes. I'm well into it.

—Excellent. As far as I can remember, it was a traveling salesman, wasn't it?

—Yes. A girl is found raped and murdered in a wooded area near a country town in Jutland. The police discover that the salesman is the last person who saw her alive. He is taken in for questioning, and after twelve hours of grilling, he is charged with the crime solely because he is the last person to have seen her. The girl was quite promiscuous, and the salesman weakens his case because at first he lies, denying that they had spent the night together. But the point is that they—the police—have got the wrong man. He isn't the one who killed her. Can you remember, we talked about calling it *The Wrong Man,* but decided that wasn't a good idea because there's a Hitchcock film by the same title.

—Right. And then you suggested, as I recall, *The Bedeviled Man,* which is an excellent title because it can be understood in more than one way, but unfortunately Panduro has already used it. What was it you suggested then?

—*No One Knows the Day.* But the trouble with that is it makes people think of Branner.

—Let's just check to see if it's been used.

Mogens Knudsen walked over to his bookshelf and looked in the current Politiken *Who Wrote What.*

—Let's see, *No Borders, No One Knows Death,* yes, it's here, unfortunately: *No One Knows the Day,* novel, 1946, Alfred Hauge, Norwegian, Danish Youth Publishing Company—it's probably some religious thing. I don't know if we can—

—Oh, I'll undoubtedly find a completely different title before I'm through. I've only just begun.

—You figure on the fall?

—Yes. I plan to deliver the manuscript around the end of June.

—It sounds very promising. I gather from what you said that suspense isn't the main thing. It's more a psychological story like *In the Same Boat,* isn't it?

—Yes, that's what I'd like it to be. What happens is that the man is first charged and imprisoned for three weeks. He can't establish an alibi; but, on the other hand, the police don't have anything on him other than that he had been with the girl and was the last person to see her. I want to try to tell a story about what could happen to anybody—what could happen to you or to me. Can you account for how you spent, let's say, last Sunday evening?

—Certainly not. I think it sounds like a good idea. Precisely the kind of thing you have a special knack for.

Bang hesitated. He had actually been thinking that the book should be different than his previous books—not only thematically, but also insofar as it portrayed people and milieux which he couldn't just take from reality but would have to use his imagination for and do research on.

—Then it happens, he continued after taking a sip of sherry, the man gets a little deed-writer of a lawyer who proves to develop tremendously with the case. After three weeks the police have to release him, but the charge is not dropped. The police continue investigating the case, convinced, despite everything, that they got the right man in the first place. But after three more weeks they have to drop the charges because of insufficient evidence. Now, maybe *there's* a title: *Insufficient Evidence?*

—Just a minute, we can look it up. Yes, that's all right—here's an *Insufficient Understanding* and an *Insufficient Link,* but "evidence" is still available.

—I just have a rough outline of the rest, but what happens is that his wife leaves him and no one believes he is innocent; so he is forced to prove his own innocence. He goes to the country town and takes upon himself, so to say, the job of detective.

—And does he find the real murderer?

—That's what I had originally planned. But perhaps the ending

42

would be more powerful if he never did find the real murderer and had to live under suspicion the rest of his life. Of course, that would disappoint all the readers who are looking forward to a solution of the mystery.

—I can see your problem. In fact, it's two completely different novels that you have to choose between. But it's only January now, so you're in good time as usual. Unless you're about to become as speedy as Straus.

Bang sat back a little in his chair. He knew what was coming. Straus had published two books last year, one in the spring and one in the fall. Now he was repeating the same trick.

—Straus brought a new manuscript today. I don't really know if I ought to tell you that, but whom would you gossip to?

—A spring book?

—Spring book? No, he turned that in back in November. But he's already begun yet another book, so the one he turned in today he talked us into publishing this summer. Then he's bringing in one more manuscript before the end of June, so that means he'll get out three books this year. There's simply no stopping him. The most fantastic thing about it is that he gets better and better—as you do.

Mogens Knudsen emptied his glass.

—Do you want a little more?

—No, thanks. I have to be running along, and you were just about to leave, after all. There was just one thing more.

—Yes?

—If you have the figures, I'd like to hear how the fall sales went.

—We can do that quickly. I have the stock summary right here. Let me see, *In the Same Boat*—I'm just adding up—we're into the fourth edition. How much did you get for the first three?

—Two thousand.

—And we're a good way into the fourth. Now, of course we have to figure that some of them may be returned, and right at the moment things are pretty quiet with clearance sales, but we've delivered fifteen hundred of the fourth edition, so it's really going swimmingly.

—Fifteen hundred—but weren't there four thousand?

—Yes, maybe we've overshot the mark a little, but we'll certainly get rid of them. Your backlist of books always sells well.

There were more things Bang wanted to ask about, but he let them go. He wanted to know if there were plans to include some of his earlier books in the book-club selections, or to reissue them in paperback, but he couldn't bring himself to broach it. He also wanted to know if his early books were selling at all, but since nothing was said about it, that undoubtedly indicated that sales were slow now. Most of all he wanted to ask how much Straus had sold during the Christmas season, but that question smacked so much of jealousy that it was impossible to ask. Besides, he more or less knew. *Stay out of Sight* was now in its sixth edition, and that meant that between twenty and thirty thousand copies must have been sold. The exact number was immaterial—Straus had clearly surpassed Bang, had probably sold twice as much.

Mogens Knudsen seemed to have guessed what Bang was thinking, for after rising a little from his seat, he sat back and pushed the sheet of the sales totals to one side.

—Disappointed? You have to expect some of your old readers to desert you when you quite deliberately—and in my opinion very cleverly—change your style. We agreed, after all, even during the outline, that *In the Same Boat* would be presented on a—what shall I say?—not a finer but another plan. We agreed that we wouldn't promise more than the book contained as far as bloodshed and that sort of thing goes. Now that you are putting more and more stress on psychological aspects, you must resign yourself to the fact that you can't continue to match your previous sales. In my opinion, four editions is an unusually good sale for a book like your last one.

Bang kept his thoughts to himself. Straus was also dealing less with murder and had become more and more "psychological." Nevertheless, he sold better and better, and now he had three novels scheduled to appear in '70, whereas Bang wasn't sure he would even finish the one he was in the middle of. And then, in addition, Straus was always getting praise and encouragement from the "highbrow" group at *Vindrosen.*

Mogens Knudsen rose from his chair—this time definitely—and began to put on his coat. Bang drained his glass, and the two men walked to the door together, but there Mogens Knudsen stopped.

—Oh, I almost forgot, but then you already know it anyway, don't you?

—What?

—Your book is going to be reviewed on the radio tonight, which should surely give your sales a bit of a shot in the arm. And by Straus, no less—that should certainly get people to turn on their radios.

—Straus is going to review my book?

—Do you think it's wrong to let one crime writer review another? Journalistically speaking, anyway, it's a splendid idea. I think if there is anyone who knows where the shoe pinches—and besides, you have to admit that the man is fantastically fair.

—And honest, Bang couldn't help but add.

—Exactly. He says what he means. It's not his way to hold back out of misguided consideration for his colleagues or out of fear that he'll be accused of feathering his own nest. But if I were you, I wouldn't be afraid of Straus. You're sure to get impartial treatment, and your book is good enough to stand up to that, in my opinion at least. Listen, why don't you stop in another day when I have more time, and preferably telephone ahead of time? I'm always pleased to hear how your work is going and to give you good advice if I can. You will drop in, won't you?

Bang nodded, and left the publishing house with his mind filled with thoughts of Straus. Straus who had come to the city in order to review *In the Same Boat,* who had taken the same route during the day as Bang himself, and who was now sitting at the studio recording the review. Straus' own book had been reviewed on the radio by a psychiatrist a few days after it had been published, and this review had developed into a long debate in the newspapers, which Bang had followed only through the headlines.

The thought of Straus at the radio station preoccupied Bang entirely. Straus calm and relaxed as always, with his manuscript in front of him on the green desk, or perhaps with just a few notes, for Straus' best mode of presentation was oral, and it would be just like him to improvise his talk while still scrupulously observing the time limit. The few times that Straus condescended to attend a meeting at the Poe Club, he had invariably given short elegant speeches without the aid of a single note.

Bang bought a newspaper to check the radio schedule. The book review was scheduled for a quarter past ten and it was now a little after five. There were five hours before he would turn on the radio and hear what Straus could find to say about *In the Same Boat.* Bang threw the paper away and walked to his car.

On his way to the car he decided that there would undoubtedly be another parking ticket stuck under his windshield wiper—that was the kind of day it was—but there wasn't. On the other hand, it was impossible to move the car because a delivery truck had double-parked next to him. The truck was not locked and Bang opened the door, released the hand brake, and began pushing it. It was a difficult job, and he was sweating profusely by the time he heard the discomfiting sound of the truck bumping into the car in front of it, which was double-parked also. Bang walked around the delivery truck and saw that he had smashed a taillight of the car in front. He stood there at a loss for a moment, and then went back to his own car to find a pen and something to write on, but he had scarcely slid in behind the steering wheel before someone knocked on his window.

—Come out here a minute.

Bang hurriedly rummaged around in the glove compartment to indicate to the man that he was searching for a pen and a piece of paper.

—I've already written down your license number. There's no use trying to get away.

Bang rolled down the window.

—I was just trying to . . .

—And another thing. Do you have business at the British Embassy? That's a beautiful car you're driving around in, but it doesn't have diplomatic plates as far as I can see.

Bang shut the glove compartment and started the car. The thought of Straus at the radio station still filled his consciousness, and he couldn't face an argument.

—Hey, there! Hey!

In order to get out of the parking place, Bang had to back his car up a little; the man followed. Bang had the car in reverse and tried to steer with one hand while he rolled the window up again with the other. When he had got the window all the way up, the man ran in front of the car and positioned himself there. Bang let the car roll forward a little, but when the man made no sign of moving, he gave it up and switched off the ignition. The man kept standing there with his arms crossed until Bang climbed out. A group of people had collected on the sidewalk to observe the scene.

The man turned to one of the onlookers:

—Would you mind going into the British Embassy and asking if this gentleman had business there?

The onlooker hesitated a little.

—The license number is MB 461102. And perhaps we could get the name at the same time.

—My name is Bang, Bang began, and I didn't have an errand at the embassy. I had no idea that this was an embassy parking place.

—And of course you weren't trying to take off just now, either, were you?

—No.

Before Bang had got a chance to write his name on a piece of paper, the owner of the damaged car and the delivery-truck driver had showed up, and while he negotiated with them—the truck driver also discovered damage to his vehicle—a man from the British Embassy showed up. Bang had to write down his license number, his name, and his address on three different forms before the man would let him go. His whole body had begun trembling, and he barely managed to avoid damaging another car when he was finally allowed to maneuver out of his parking place. A short way down the street he pulled over to the curb, got a little bottle of Valium out of the glove compartment, and took two tablets, swallowing them as best he could without water. Then he drove around haphazardly for a while, and since his whole body was still trembling and since he knew from experience that the pills required half an hour to take effect, he started to look for a new parking place.

The worst of the rush hour was not over yet, and it took a long time to find a place—this time it had to be legal. He finally found one that was big enough for his altogether too big car, turned off the ignition, and clipped and lit a cigar—he had thrown away the Gyldendal cigar during the argument with the three men. After he had taken a few puffs on his cigar and had sat for a little while trying to calm down, he opened the door and climbed out. He was hungry, but there weren't any restaurants nearby. There was a little bar, however, and he went in and got a beer—the second drink of the day. After a while he felt fairly calm and went out to the car again. Now he wanted to find a place to eat, and he hoped he would be lucky enough to meet someone he could talk to, as he felt like telling somebody about (and thereby minimizing) his troubles.

Entering the Drop Inn, he stopped. Straus was in the city, and he recalled meeting Straus here once. In the front cloakroom hung a large-checked tweed coat with sheepskin lining which suddenly he thought he recognized as Straus'. Thinking it over more carefully—on the way to the Cheval Blanc—he decided that Straus didn't go to the Drop Inn any more. Of late, Straus had been cultivating a reputation as a gourmet and, as a guest writer, supplied recipes to *Politiken*. If he stayed in the city for dinner, he undoubtedly went to one of the better eating places. But Bang was now in Mikkel Bryggers Street and he went into the Cheval Blanc after casting a sidelong glance at the cloakroom, which didn't reveal any coats which looked like Straus'.

There was no one he knew in the restaurant, and he ordered kidneys and a mug of half-and-half. He had nearly finished the beer by the time the meal came, and he ordered another. The yellow Valium pills had now taken effect and he began to feel relaxed. While he ate, he leafed through a newspaper.

My I.B.M. (one would think they paid me for mentioning it) hums impatiently; on top of the typing element I read that I am writing with Delegate type, and I sit here wondering why I've come to a standstill right here. Have I used up everything that I fed my subconscious last night? Is it because I've counted the pages lying in front of the typewriter (as each page is finished I let the typewriter spit it out and it floats down beautifully on top of the others) and have discovered that I'm already on the eighth—which could be called a good day's work? Is it because I feel that details are getting the upper hand now and obstructing the goal? Or is it simply because I have been thinking of Copenhagen—Copenhagen during rush hour on a winter evening, when the working day is over and you start looking for a place to eat —and want to forget Bang for a bit while I go out into the city myself?

I delay dinner a little and go to the Walking Street to look at the girls and the shops. It's cold and I walk briskly in order to keep warm. The shops are about to close, and people have packages in their arms. I walk up to the Raadhusplads, look down toward Vesterbro Street, walk out into the middle of the square and read the announcements and news bulletins spelled out on the electric sign around the top of the Politiken Building. The Raadhus clock strikes six; I sit down on a bench and button up my coat collar under my chin so I won't get cold. Maybe I should go across the square and eat at Frascati's this evening for a change. That was where I ate with my parents and my older brother—all three are dead now—when I was confirmed (not in a church confirmation, nor in a civil confirmation either, but they thought it should be celebrated anyway). Then there's the Queen's Pub or the King Frederik. And there is the restaurant in the S.A.S. hotel, and there is the Imperial, and there is a good Chinese restaurant a short distance down Vesterbro Street.

The food here is excellent, for that matter, and though I don't look down on Danish food (I'm not a gourmet like Straus), that is not what I miss. If I miss anything like that, it is, paradoxically enough, Danish —yes, prepare for a shock—cigars. Maybe they're not very good, but I'm used to them, and I can't really get used to Henry Clay or Romeo y Giulietta (which I've tried for a change, but I can't taste the difference). A cigar can have too much of a taste, too—not after a good dinner, but while one is working. Now and then I feel like having a cheroot, but you just can't get them here.

The typewriter has spat out a new page, and I won't go any further with Bang today. Now and then I wonder if I am laying it on too thick. It definitely should be one of Bang's unlucky days, but I'm afraid of losing credibility and am considering limiting myself to one traffic mishap. Either the ticket or the argument. I'll probably cut out one of the episodes (and yet the truth is that one could easily in the course of one day . . . but the truth in this context must be subordinated to credibility).

It has rained today, and I've been writing in my room with the door open so I could hear the sound of the rain falling on my veranda. Now the sun is shining again, but it's cooler than it usually is here in the middle of the day, and I think I'll go for a walk along the shore. There's a place there where the hotels leave off, and I've never got that far. Maybe I'll even take a swim before I come back.

It's the sixteenth of February and I'm planning to go swimming. I wonder if there is still frost in Denmark. It's two o'clock now, and if it's overcast in Copenhagen, it won't be long until twilight. But it is February, and the days are getting noticeably longer. One could imagine that there's a blackbird singing in Bang's larch tree.

Here there are no birds. It took me a few days before I realized it.

February Seventeenth

Dreamed a dream last night which, in its mixture of daytime reminiscences and small uncomplicated symbols, was so simple I'm almost ashamed to write it down. I'm hunting with my brother (as I wrote yesterday, I no longer recall under what pretext and don't want to check back) and we are shooting at blackbirds in a larch tree: Bang's blackbirds in Bang's larch tree. My nightly fantasies of handling hunting rifles would get L. started in a hurry. For him, none of my dreams are mysterious—everything symbolizes something else; you only need to give him a few seconds.

Another daytime reminiscence: We were out hunting—and now the accounts begin to balance uncomfortably well—I don't need L. to convince me that there's a meaning in what I dream. Because who is it I have added to the hunting party? Who else but Straus? And then all we have to do is add a few equations of the type L. excels in: Straus glides into place instead of my brother, and the bird becomes . . . I'm not exactly sure on this point, but either the consummate crime novel which we have yet to write, or else a woman (there's no mistaking the rifle, but as a kind of extension of the arm it can also symbolize the ability to write).

The strange thing is that this bird hunt takes place at Baunebakke, which my brother never visited (he died in a shooting accident at the Almegaard base in 1954). We are standing next to the house and shooting down toward the woods. When we turn back—my brother has hit the bird, not I—I aim at him. And now once more it's one of these bad dreams I have almost every night. I walk behind him, and he doesn't know that I have him in my sights. Somehow or other, Baunebakke isn't really Baunebakke, but rather the sum of a series of summer houses we've lived in together as children. He keeps on walking in front of me, and I wish he'd turn around and discover that I'm walking right behind him, aiming at him.

For L. all this would still be very simple, and maybe it is—maybe L. is right, though sometimes I've suspected him of being a little bit crazy. I've identified myself with Bang (natural at this stage of the novel) and I've identified my brother (who should have been a big brother; he was a little brother) with Straus. The weapon serves to symbolize everything there is between the two of them, and the bird is also symbolic. Not only that, L. is not surprised that nearly all my dreams wander off in houses that change while I walk through them. But now I can't really follow it any further because L. says that the houses symbolize women. Has it perhaps something to do with the fact that you "move into them"? Sometimes when I sit (sat) across from L., I would feel very insecure. The man didn't know doubt—I could never surprise him with my dreams. My house dream, where I moved from house to house and the houses changed in the course of the dream and expanded and became populated with my parents and my brother (how much better it would have been if he'd been a big brother) and with family members who had either borrowed features from each other or were pure products of fantasy (since my family is quickly exhausted)—my house dream could be explained away before you could say Cock Robin—the houses were women, didn't I know that?

A strange glint comes into L.'s eyes when he explains my dreams to me. I myself believe most in day reminiscences, but he believes in symbols. He leans forward a little and asks: Have you ever thought about how drivers behave on the highway? Have you ever seen how they tailgate each other? I hurriedly break in and explain that I always maintain a good distance from the next car, but that doesn't stop him a second. These people who pass—where one hazardously tailgates the car in front of him and afterward swings right in front of it—are *homosexuals.* One takes the other from behind, and afterward is taken himself. It sounds like gibberish to me, but I'm not the one who's the expert; and when I suddenly (for the first time) violently protest something he's said and insist upon a more practical explanation (for me, traffic is the perfect symbol—not primarily for anything erotic, but for the competitive society), he smiles and makes a note of the fact that at last I've contradicted him: it's a sign of something or other, presumably that he's hit a sensitive spot. That's the good thing about his method—if you protest, you simply corroborate what he has to say. And he goes on to ask if you've thought about the fact that cars are even equipped with exhaust pipes in the rear, and that's something to consider, after all.

Yes, he has an easy time of it. I explain to him that I've never had, don't ever remember having had, homosexual dreams. Fine—so I don't have homosexual dreams; but everybody else does, if I understand him correctly, and my refusing to have them (or to remember them) is right in line with my refusing to take his traffic theory seriously and my quick substitution of a less complicated theory. Denials don't affect him. It doesn't matter how I react to his theories or what I dream about or don't dream about, the result is the same. One day he asks me if he ever appears in my dreams, and when I truthfully say no, he becomes very thoughtful—just as thoughtful, I'd guess, as if I'd lied to him and led him to believe that I dreamed about him every night. His theories are geared to corroborate themselves no matter what I answer, and maybe that's the reason I never told him that as a child I played dolls with my neighbor's daughter and when we were alone I borrowed her clothes and we played at nursing her dolls together. It wouldn't have changed his prognosis, but he was nice about writing prescriptions, and I miss him.

I walk behind my brother through the house, keeping him in my sights, while the house changes and becomes a variation of our childhood home, and later changes again to a variation of my own house, and finally becomes my bungalow here at the hotel. At one point my parents are standing somewhere out of focus and my brother turns around. It doesn't frighten him that I'm aiming at him with the rifle, and, half awake, I tell myself that he can only die once, after all, and my parents are dead too, so they can't prevent me from shooting him. But I'm not trying to keep him in my sights in order to shoot him. He turns around again, and we're back at Baunebakke (the dream is elliptical) and when he asks me for the rifle, which is larger than a usual rifle—practically a bazooka—I hand it to him, and he opens a door and goes outside again, and down at the edge of the woods is the larch tree again, and perched in it a huge bird, and he shoots and hits the bird with the first shot, and there's no longer a bird in the tree, but now I'm about to wake up and know that they're all gone—I am here, and I am alone.

Just as the dream incorporates daytime reminiscences, the day incorporates dream reminiscences, and now I've fallen into a reverie about two elements from my dream which have no connection with each other outside the dream: my brother and Baunebakke. My brother, who took his degree while I drifted from one field of study to another; who married and made my parents grandparents—they were dead before I even got married. Who died in a meaningless accident in some sort of military training and therefore never got to read a single one of my books. Neither my parents nor he. Is it Goethe (I notice there's something about the diary form that prompts me to quote, and then I don't have a chance in the world of verifying the quotations) who writes about dead friends? They don't hear (I don't dare quote it in German) the songs that follow . . . Well, it wasn't songs that I wrote, but I can dream that they had been allowed to read at least one of my books. I can imagine having driven from the publishers with a stack of courtesy copies, and letting them be my first real readers. I think they would have understood the confession which every book is for me. I think it could have been the beginning of something new. Maybe it's hard to understand when the book in question is about murder and solving murders, but I believe we would have found a new point of contact there, my brother and I; I believe his joy in mechanical things (it was a pleasure to see him take a rifle apart and reassemble it) would have extended to the mechanics of crime intrigue. He would have been one of my good critics.

I imagine the frost, which came to Denmark in November, still there. I imagine the earth covered with snow. In my mind I take a trip to Baunebakke, past Klint's Grocery, past the church, past the country school, and then up into the hills until you can't go any farther because of the snowdrifts. The last part of the trip I make on foot, past Essmann's farm and through hollows where the snow is so deep it comes up under my trousers and down into my socks with every step. At the top of the ridge I stop and look back over the patch of trees and over Arre Lake, which has been frozen for many months. It's too far away to see whether any skaters have returned out on the ice today.

I keep on going, and now it looks as if the hills stop and the forest begins; but there's one more summer cottage, Baunebakke. I pass the little sign which is constantly getting knocked down or removed (deep down I understand them well), the little sign saying PRIVATE. And now the road (no car tracks; no one has been able to drive up here for months) winds in among the trees and there's the little cluster of log cabins with orange shutters and unbarked shingles on most of the roofs. No human footprints in the snow, only animal tracks. I go around the kitchen house, find the key on the ladder, and let myself into the main house, where I light up the stove. In a little while I'll take a long walk in the woods, and later I'll drive down to the village and eat dinner at the inn.

There are no odors here in this heat. It could be that there's something wrong with my sense of smell, but there isn't, because when I lean over my typewriter I can smell my typewriter ribbon clearly. My typewriter smells, and my coffee and cigars smell, but the place itself doesn't have any smell. I've never thought about it before, but palm trees don't have the least smell. In the living room at Baunebakke it smells the same, summer and winter; and if the smell is a little weaker on a winter day, you bring it back in a hurry by just lighting a fire in the fireplace. The woods retain their summer smell too—even in the freezing weather it's still there, and it's the same smell.

Today I'd like to trade my evening walk along the beach for a walk in a wood, but I have no idea whether they have woods here, and if they do, there probably aren't any paths in them. I'd like to have snow crunching under my shoes, and here I sit in sandals whose soles quickly become as hot as the flagstones they're supposed to protect my feet from. I'd also like to go skating, and, paradoxically, that wish could be fulfilled by taking a bus or a taxi into the city, but it would be under conditions which would just make me miss Arre Lake even more. In a hall with artificial ice and booming loudspeaker waltzes to skate in time to. So I'd rather stay here and dream about a North Zealand walk in frosty weather.

L. once said that the problem wasn't whether I could find someone who would be fond of me, but whether I could find someone I was fond of. I believe I later demonstrated to excess that I could, but there are many kinds of love, and love of things is also love. Last night I dreamed about a person whom I was fond of, though perhaps I seldom showed it (it was his fault too), and now I sit here dreaming about a thing I'm fond of: a summer cottage hidden in the snow just behind the first trees.

I could have saved myself the price of the expensive radio. The salesman said it could pick up Japan, and maybe it can, but it can't pick up Denmark. There are many short-wave stations on it, and I've turned the dial slowly through all of them, mostly at night when I figured the chances were best, but the closest I've come was that very first night when one station suddenly played Lumbye's "Amelie Waltz"; but that wasn't a Danish station, and heaven knows how they happened to play that particular tune.

I'd like to hear more Lumbye, I'd like to hear Danish voices, news from home, but first and foremost I'd like to hear whether there is still frost in Denmark.

February Eighteenth

While he ate he leafed through the day's papers. *B.T.* had an announcement of the radio program under the headline STRAUS ABOUT BANG. The brief item was illustrated with a picture of Straus, a slightly older picture from the time when he was experimenting with a full beard.

Bang purposely took his time, since he didn't have to see his accountant until eight o'clock. All the same, it turned out that he drove out of the city too early and had to wait a quarter of an hour for Madsen on a little landing outside the accountant's office in Vangede while an actor's voice he recognized went through endless possibilities of tax deductions with Madsen. They ran over their appointment time, and Bang went downstairs, where he got permission to use the telephone and called Erik Balling. The actor's voice—it was certainly Henning Moritzen—had reminded him that *In the Same Boat* was still under consideration at Nordic Films.

Balling was home, and Bang asked him if he had read the short synopsis of the novel which Bang had written, in which the original plot had been altered quite radically—out of consideration of the fact that too many people already knew how the novel ended and could do with a surprise in the new version. Balling had read it and was favorably inclined, but said there was plenty of time. Just today he had (Bang now knew what was coming) had a visit from Straus, only a quick visit to drop off the finished adaptation of *Stay out of Sight.*

Balling had set aside the next few weeks to write the scenario, Bahs had already begun designing the set, and they hoped to begin filming by early March. Of course *In the Same Boat* would also be filmed, but it would undoubtedly have to wait until next year. Which shouldn't prevent Bang from coming out to have a light lunch with Balling one of these days and talk over the alterations in the story. Balling was not completely convinced that they were all for the better.

Bang was called in to see the accountant. The actor had gone, and an hour's concentrated work followed. Madsen offered Bang a glass of port and a little cigar—he himself smoked cheroots, and the office was soon stiflingly thick with cigar smoke. First Madsen added up Bang's income on an adding machine and looked incredulously at the result.

—How much did you figure it out to be?

—I haven't added it up at all.

—I see. Well, we'll have to find some deductions. You've earned thirty-two thousand dollars. It's really quite a jump from last year, so even if six thousand is so-called tax-free, you're in for a real blow some time or other. I've had the bank send me your statement of assets as you requested, and before we go on, I just want to suggest that you take some serious steps toward investing your money better. It's ridiculous to have all that money invested in bonds, and then besides that you have a lot of money sitting in your checking account which isn't collecting interest. Look, bonds have depreciated so much this year that the loss nearly cancels out the dividends when you figure in your tax. Personally, I think bonds are going to depreciate even more in '70, so if I were you, I'd sell them and buy mortgages or stocks first thing in the morning. But first and foremost, I'd do something about your checking account—there's nearly seven thousand dollars in it, which is just sheer madness. Haven't you considered buying a larger house? Houses are the only things that continually increase in value, and moreover you can deduct your debt from your taxes. Also, I'd get a nice fat life-insurance policy, which is also deductible.

Madsen filled Bang's glass to the brim, and they began to go over the deductions.

—Have you done any traveling this year? I have an author who earns even more than you do, but his net income is smaller because he has a huge debt on his property, and in addition he travels continually. Recently he was on a safari in Africa, and he wrote just one article on shooting elephants for *Politiken,* and now we are deducting the entire trip. Wouldn't you like to take a trip somewhere? I hear that you're on your own again—couldn't you take a trip around the world or something? Travel to some place where there's a lot of sunshine?

—I write best at home. Besides, I haven't the least desire to shoot elephants.

—You have a summer cottage. How about buying a larger one?

They began to discuss other possible deductions. Bang's head felt heavy. He let his cigar lie there half smoked and didn't touch the port. It could have been the heavy cigar smoke in the office, but it also could have been the mixture of a couple of Valium pills with what he had drunk. He had no doubt as to who had been in Africa shooting elephants, and caught himself wondering whether Straus had also managed to make a visit to Madsen in the course of the day. In the end he couldn't keep from interrupting Madsen, who was saying that Bang should buy a tape-recorder and his own photo-copy machine and replace his typewriter in order to get more deductions.

—Has Straus been here today?

—Straus? No, he never comes himself. His wife takes care of everything for him. She just sends it all here, and then we deal with it by telephone. Why do you ask?

—I assume it was Straus on the safari.

—Yes. He has, by the way, another gimmick—might be an idea for you. You know, I'm sure, that he's a gastronomer. At the moment everything he eats is research for a kind of cookbook that he's writing. We're trying to see if we can get away with deducting all of it. I'm really sorry that you can't think of more deductions—what we have here is nothing.

They eventually got the deductions totaled up and the property forms and statement of assets figured out. Bang put his signature on the still blank tax statement and passed it across the table to Madsen, who lit a new cheroot with his old one because he had run out of matches.

—Yes, one ought to be an author, Madsen said. But you and Straus are exceptions, of course. In the old days it was only my actors who came with any really large tax statements. How does it happen, anyway, that suddenly a couple of writers are well up in the five-figure income bracket? Are people reading more books? I myself haven't the strength for anything more than television.

—We're probably more industrious than they were in the old days. And then there's so much else we do. There's radio and television and newspapers and lectures. As you can see, I have over twenty statements of earnings this year.

Madsen leaned back a little in his chair and puffed at his cheroot, which he hadn't got really going.

—How does one come up with a story like *In the Same Boat,* anyway? Do you just suddenly get the idea, or is it something that you go around working out in your mind for months or maybe even years? Do you yourself know how it will end when you begin it?

—I have the entire plan before I start.

—And of course you've already started a new one? And you already know who the murderer is?

—This time the whole idea is that the murderer is never found.

—And last time you let him go free. It's true I said I don't have strength for anything more than television, but I always read you and Straus. Don't you think people would rather have the murderer caught and punished in the end?

—You may be right. But the idea of *In the Same Boat* was that the murderer would be punished by his own guilty conscience. I think it would have been a liberation for him to be caught, and in a way he actually goes around hoping that someone will expose him.

—Well, I really didn't catch that point. To change the subject: it suddenly occurred to me that you have income from abroad, too.

—Yes, but that's taxed there, isn't it?

—Well, that varies from country to country. Don't you have some correspondence so we can check on the matter?

—I'm afraid I've thrown it all away. It's been such a confused year with my separation and all.

—I see.

Madsen looked thoughtful.

—It may well cause you certain unpleasantness if . . . Well, let's forget it; it isn't really tax fraud. After all, you can just say you thought all the tax on the money had been paid at one time if the tax bureau comes up with anything. Or do you think we should try to dig out the figures? I think we should.

Bang hesitated a moment.

—You're obviously entertaining the principle that crime pays, Madsen said, smiling.

—Aside from the matter of conscience.

—Yes, and that I won't meddle with.

—I'm quite sure that the tax on the money has been paid. If not, it's up to the tax bureau to figure it out.

—Very well. It's your decision. I'll fill out your income-tax statement and send it to City Hall and a copy to you.

Madsen got up.

—But remember what I said. The banks open tomorrow at nine thirty. Sell your bonds and take out all that capital you have sitting in your checking account, where it's not collecting any interest. In the meantime, I'll try to find some good mortgages for you. If I were you, I'd buzz off to the Bahamas right away. I don't know what it is about Danish winters; they get worse and worse, it seems to me.

Bang drove home and let himself into his empty house. It was nine thirty; there was still at least an hour before he would hear the review on the radio. He paced somewhat restlessly around the room, and turned the heat up and then down again. He had forgotten to switch off his typewriter, and it had got very warm standing and humming all day. Next to the machine lay the morning's writing, which he pushed to the back of the desk—that was the last thing in the world he wanted to look at now. He glanced at the pile of unpaid bills and pushed them a little farther out of sight too. The house smelled of the morning's cigars, and he opened a few windows. The kitchen was quite a mess; he took two Codymagnylers and washed them down with a beer from the refrigerator before he started to clean up.

He could smell the odor of the day's numerous cigars permeating his clothes and went into the bathroom to take a hot bath. Whereas the rest of the house bore the stamp of Nadja's departure, she was still present in the bathroom; the smell of her perfume remained as if the tiles were able to hold on to it. At the bottom of the bathroom cupboard were some of her cotton and a comb she had forgotten to take with her. He threw them both out before he sank down into the filled tub.

The bath made him sleepy. While he dried himself, he drank a fresh beer. It was a little past ten, and he turned on the clock radio in the bedroom. He considered getting dressed again, but chose instead to put on his pajamas and get into bed. He set the beer on the bedtable and laid two Noludar sleeping pills beside it. After he had crept down under the quilt, he swallowed the two pills and turned off the lamp, so that the only light came from the dial on the radio.

A poet was giving a review of another poet's work, and Bang only half listened. His headache would not let up, and even though his body felt sleepy, he was aware that the day's many conversations were continuing in his head, and that the Noludar pills didn't work nearly as promptly as they had done in the beginning. Straus was sitting at his country estate waiting, like Bang, beside a radio. Or was he so busy now that he no longer had time to listen to himself on the radio? There was no end to the poet's enthusiasm for his colleague; finally he raised his voice and said: "I could talk much more about these poems, but my time is about to run out, so I will put it very briefly. With these poems the seventies began."

Straus' review is giving me problems, and I need to get a better grip on Straus himself before I tackle it. Last night I took (sleepless) time and courage to read through what I've already written, and the "invisible" characters disturb me. I must restrain my irony toward Straus —it's on the verge of being too much of a good thing, what with elephant hunts and the country estate—he doesn't resemble a real writer any more. I've determined to dupe the enemy, and I've done

61

it damned poorly up to now. I've followed my usual technique of piecing things together from all sorts of models, but I have the feeling that the different pieces fall apart, so one might say that what Straus "is" is a strange piecemeal work. For the time being, I'll even out the balance by making Straus' review fairer than I had originally intended —assuming also that the fairer it is, the worse. My irony makes Straus a lesser figure, and the point is precisely that Straus shall be frightfully great. I'm very tempted to postpone Straus' review a little, but my experience tells me (and you can't teach an old dog new tricks) that I must write the book in the same sequence that it is going to be read.

The business about Nadja is wrong, too. Here the problem is different: I introduce her too late. And it's a mistake that I don't see how I can correct as long as I've arranged the beginning of the book according to the principle "Bang's day until . . ." This means I have only one or two scenes in which to present Nadja. Well, I could let Bang think about her throughout the day, but I don't like these flashbacks, and the story already drags catastrophically. This is something I'll have to think about some more.

The little scene I wrote for my own enjoyment about Bang and Nadja in the bathroom and in bed was certainly not very clear, but what good will it do to rewrite it when it won't be included in the book? Nevertheless, I've thought about revising it. The idea is that Nadja has already had intercourse and doesn't have anything against doing it again, but she lacks the patience to make a big production out of it. Bang may well have a suspicion about this, though the point is intended for the reader, of course. Perhaps something could be done with the very last lines.

I wrote:

"They toast one another, and her eyes have a special luster that tells him she is feeling good right now."

One could add:

". . . whether it was due to the bath, their intercourse . . ." (That's a little too technical.) ". . . the good red wine or something else entirely." Possibly: "Or something else entirely which he didn't know about." But the latter is certainly spelling things out a bit too obviously. In any case, the scene is definitely not going to be included in the book, and that's what worries me.

Murder is a serious business, and I can't just fall back on biopharmacology. I want to bring in Bang's jealousy (and not simply his loneliness) at a much earlier point, but I can't see how to do it without upsetting the whole plan. Can I let him call her up? Can she come to get something she has forgotten? No, it all has to happen inside Bang, and unfortunately that's not where my strength lies. A (kindly disposed, for a change) colleague once called me a behaviorist, and, strangely enough, he thought there should be some writers like that, though he himself writes symbolic poetry. When I get to the behavioristic jealousy, I shall certainly, if all goes well, be able to handle it. But right now I lack the means to describe Bang's jealousy, because my predisposition leads me to put Nadja to one side until it's time for her to be made use of.

Medically, I have more than covered myself. Bang has drunk two glasses of sherry at Gyldendal and one at his accountant's. He had drunk one beer at a bar, two beers before he went to bed, and two half-and-halfs at the Cheval Blanc. He has taken two tablets (five milligrams) of Valium, two of Codymagnyler (ten milligrams of codein phosphate) and two sleeping pills.

And the day is far from finished yet.

February Twentieth

The local drugstore (for want of a pharmacy) teems with pills and preparations you can pluck right off the shelves—prescriptions are unknown here. They make a big deal out of packaging and have invented the most enticing names. Stood for a long time in the store and vacillated between Serenal, Notturno, Tranquibril, Equinase, Dormison, and a great many others. The clerks are of no use—they are ready to swear that all of them will cure whatever you have. Serenal sounded as if it could make you peaceful, and though the pills in the yellow bottle turned out to be cyclamen-colored, I let my choice fall on them. Not in order to sleep—my sleeping problem overshadows all my other problems—but in order to stop speculating about whether I could fall asleep when I have taken the actual sleeping pills. And what should they be? I went by the names and pounced upon Dormison and Notturno. Dormison is a kind of syrup you dilute in water (nothing there about how large a portion); Notturno is a little two-colored plastic capsule which is very hard to swallow.

The experiments with the local sleeping medicines have cost me a night's sleep and another day's work. This time I tried not to mix them with alcohol, but it went all wrong anyway. Serenal had a good enough deadening effect, but at the same time made my mouth so dry that I had to gulp down several glasses of water. After I'd lain down a little and read (I've gotten hold of H. C. Andersen's fairy tales in a hideously illustrated and much abridged edition, not to mention the impossible translation into English), I poured two teaspoons of Dormison into a glass of water and gulped down the pasty result. After an hour I had not become either more or less sleepy, and after another hour I concluded that I wouldn't risk anything by trying the last remedy I had at my disposal above and beyond the other two.

The effect hit me promptly, full force. My heart began to hammer, and when I began taking my pulse, it rose rapidly. If it wasn't for the fact that Notturno immediately doubles your pulse (but that *could* naturally be the combination with other things) it would be a wonderful sleeping remedy, for it was most like being hammered over the head with a shovel.

I lay down for a few hours and at regular intervals took my pulse, which swung between 110 and 140. At last I yielded to the temptation to knock my pulse down with a new dose of Serenal and got a new siege of thirst. With a banging headache and a pulse of 110, read H. C. Andersen until the letters began to blur. Came upon a mysterious fairy tale that my parents had never read to me when I was a child, "Aunt Toothache," and felt totally disoriented. Either there was something wrong with the translation, or it was a very mysterious fairy tale, or I was more beside myself than I felt. Fell into a kind of half-sleep when it began to get light and once again dreamed I shot at targets with my brother. We were both dressed up in the finest hunting costumes, went down Brante Hill in deep snow in fog during the thaw, and just as my brother walks in front of me, without wishing to I raise my gun, aim, and shoot him down. The dream is in color and an enormous quantity of blood quickly spreads in all directions around him until the floor of the forest is covered with red snow. So there is something for the little dream interpreter to think over (but I think that L. would certainly have preferred it to be my father I had shot down).

Went around all day beside myself, didn't dare take any more pills (for my head) and couldn't force anything down in the heat. Broke a promise and whiled away the rest of the afternoon with thin whiskeys. Threw away my new medicine, went to bed early, and went to sleep on a solid dose of bourbon direct from the bottle.

I don't know why I slept so poorly—i.e., I well know why, but there are many reasons, and I don't know which one is the most important. I don't know whether I'm more afraid of falling asleep or of not falling asleep. L. says that people are afraid of falling asleep because they are afraid of dying. But he also says (sometimes he isn't too original) that people aren't afraid of dying, they are afraid of . . . guess what yourself. I'm afraid of not sleeping because I know how things go for me the next day. At the same time I'm afraid of sleeping because I have bad dreams. I hate to lose control of my consciousness. Then there's the question, Why do I have bad dreams? Because I write, and because I'm approaching something difficult. I don't have the faintest idea of how I'll cope with Straus' radio review, and after that there are things much, much worse. I shouldn't think about the next day's work just before I go to bed, but I can't help it. Sometime I'll try to write a nice little love novel without a single murder. Then I'll probably lose all my readers, but maybe I'll be able to sleep at night again. Doubt the last for that matter—it's too late. And so we're home again: Self-Portrait of the Writer as Martyr.

My trip to the city yesterday had another purpose, by the way— I wanted to go to the barber shop. My hair has got much too long for this heat, and the first time I plugged in my electric razor, it burned out, although I had carefully shifted it to 110 volts, so I'm well on my way to a full beard. And I still am, because in the door of the barber shop I turned back. Why should it be the sole right of women to change their type now and then? Granted, all this hair and beard is a plague in the heat, but it is fun to appear different. As a child I loved carnivals, and it's carnival time. There will be a big carnival in the city on Saturday, and when they hold a carnival in these parts, it's really a carnival. There's also a ball at the hotel this evening after the big pageant, and the porter, uninvited, has approached me (as if it really didn't occur to him that I keep to myself) and offered to rent me a costume. I have no desire to go to the ball, but I suddenly got the desire to wear a costume. What should I be? I've a few days to think it over. It probably won't come to anything, but it might be fun to go out on an expedition in a carnival costume.

A comedy in school was my literary debut, and since I wrote it myself, I was also in the position to assign myself the leading role. I played a gentleman thief who incessantly disguised himself as different characters in order not to be recognized. The world didn't lose any great actor—my first part was also my last, but I was competent, and I believe I was never more obsessed by any task than I was by playing the metamorphosis part I had written for myself. Mother sewed all my costumes according to my directions, and I was my own makeup man. Perhaps that was the road I should have taken.

I didn't go into the barber shop; I turned around in the doorway; I still have my long hair and full beard. Though I seldom dare venture out into the sun and even more seldom without my hat, my face has got brown. I stand before the mirror (something my main characters are never allowed to do) and observe myself. The heat has taken away my appetite; I've lost fifteen pounds and have become hollow-cheeked. I brush my receding hair over my temples and put on my sunglasses.

Things have gone surprisingly quickly. I am nearly unrecognizable.

66

February Twenty-first

STRAUS' REVIEW (attempt)

Let me take the bull by the horns right away and admit that I'm a colleague and perhaps even a competitor of Bang. It would be the easiest and by far most becoming thing to act like a loyal colleague and praise Bang for his new novel, *In the Same Boat*. It's not a bad book either, so I wouldn't violate my conscience by letting it go at that. But to begin with the conclusion—on the other hand, I don't think the book is good enough, and I want to break through all this, to cancel my membership in the usual Danish mutual-admiration society, and then take the thrashing as well as the suspicion of having been out to feather my own nest.

In the Same Boat is no ordinary crime novel. We constantly follow the main character, get to know a little about his thoughts—only a little: Bang purposely doesn't probe deeply. The suspense lies not in what *has* happened, but in what *will* happen. I won't give away the whole plot—that would be a shame because there should be a few surprises to look forward to—but I can certainly venture to tell a little. The main character is a careerist in the Foreign Ministry, a typical representative of what we call the "Establishment" and at the same time a victim of it, a man without attributes, as Robert Musil calls such people. He drinks too much at a party, he goes to bed with a girl, and afterward drives her home. The car ends up in a ditch, and Brun —Bang's main characters always have names that begin with B, and there's certainly supposed to be a great deal of color symbolism in the name—convinces the girl to get behind the wheel and take responsibility for the accident when the police arrive. The first time around, Brun manages to avoid difficulties with the police, but the matter isn't so easily disposed of.

The girl has Brun under her thumb, and she's not long in taking advantage of it. She begins to extort money from him, she threatens to wreck his private life—his conventional marriage—and she threatens to destroy his career. She is his extreme opposite, just as hippie as he is square. One soon guesses that he'll eventually rub her out, and the guess is correct. Bang is a tight-plot man, but he seldom has any surprises up his sleeve. How Brun gets rid of the girl and what happens after that, I won't reveal—it would be a shame to do so—but the conclusion only toys with the unconventional. The respectable Brun escapes indictment; but crime does not pay anyway because Bang emphasizes Brun's guilty conscience and flirts with the old theme of a guilty person's longing to be exposed.

The book is entertaining and a good piece of craftsmanship, but it never really goes beneath the surface and therefore falls betwixt and between. I must admit that I prefer the old-fashioned crime novel with a murder in every other chapter, creaking doors, and a detective who assembles the suspects in the last chapter and reveals the murderer—after giving himself free rein in explaining how cunning he has been. I prefer Helle Stangerup and Else Fischer, who play the good old game after the good old rules without putting on airs and attempting to tell us something profound.

It is characteristic of Bang that he condensed his novel for serialization in a slick weekly magazine, and it is characteristic that in the serial version he suggests that the police still have a chance of nabbing Brun. Among other things, Bang writes to make money, and I do too, but one has to draw the line somewhere, and I think that Bang draws it at the wrong place.

The crime novel is flirting with "highbrow" culture these years, and it is evident that Bang has tried to incorporate a critique of existing society in his suspense novel, but he packages his critique in entertaining suspenseful situations to such a degree that I imagine it goes over the heads of most of his readers. The reader is cunningly manipulated to identify with the career man Brun, though Bang covers himself well by providing Brun with a few character defects, and even though Bang flirts with a sympathetic stance toward the hippie girl, there is nevertheless no question but that she is the villain of the novel. She is seen from the outside, as girls nearly always are in Bang's novels; this is true of Brun's wife as well. Their characterizations are hung on a few clichés—the girl smokes hash and plays beat records, the wife is a frustrated suburban housewife and drinks a little too much. In Bang's novels the women are kept at a fatal distance. It is reflected in the language, which automatically becomes slack when there are women in the offing. Let me give an example: Bang's girls always have a smell; they smell of perfume and shampoo and whatnot, but Bang never uses the word. Instead, he writes "scent", and that is characteristic of his whole attitude toward language. To put it in good plain Danish, there are simply no balls in Bang's relationship to women and to language in general.

In the Same Boat plays with the idea of the inner psychopath in the nice guy, but it is satisfied with just playing. It plays with criticism of the false values of a careerist society, but it is itself a piece of entertainment for overpressured career men and women. If this isn't evident in anything else, it's evident in the language, which is depressingly conventional. I haven't made a close comparison of the two versions, but I would guess that Bang didn't have to delete a single word for the sake of the word in his magazine adaptation. He only flirts with revolution in the language. How is one to take the following sentence: "He brushed her fine-textured hair from her neck, kissed her on the throat, and the delicate scent of her perfume entered his nostrils, while he carefully guided his free hand in under her sweater and began to caress her breast"? Why should her hair be fine-textured? Does a woman really smell only "delicately" of shampoo? And why so careful with his hands? Characteristically enough, the sentence concludes a chapter. The reader has to imagine the rest, which fades out discreetly like a Hollywood film from the forties. Bang's heroes take on their women like a nun takes on a sailor, and this being the case, I prefer, quite frankly, that one should avoid sex and write crime novels according to the good old recipe.

In all fairness to the man, Bang is good at weaving an intrigue, and his book is entertaining, but it would have been much more entertaining if it hadn't been weighed down with a lot of pretensions which it can't live up to—beginning with the title. Even the cover design is "refined": it has a scent but no smell.

We are so kind to one another in our little Denmark, and it was certainly the intention that I should be kind to Bang, but, at the risk of being accused of having an ax to grind, I've chosen to set aside all shame and state my honest opinion about a colleague and, let us add, competitor. My advice to readers is to read *In the Same Boat* because there's nothing wrong with the plot. But my advice to Bang is to sniff the women a little less and smell them a little more. Either show his hand as the first-rate writer of popular literature that he is, or go in for revolution on its own terms and begin with the language. Either that or give up and admit that his sympathy is and will remain with that middle class which he always describes and which he best describes when maintaining his loyalty toward it.

February Twenty-second

Carnival! I had really decided on my old brilliant role as gentleman thief, but suddenly I had doubts about how such a person really looked. He would, in any case, not have a nearly full-grown beard. Decided instead, after almost having driven the clerk mad—all these roles, the possibilities—to be Don Juan, the ladies' man. Here the full beard shows to good advantage and somehow I can certainly imagine myself a sunburned seducer of Donna Anna, Donna Elvira, and poor little Zerlina. It is, of course, Mozart's Don Juan as I have tried to capture him from memory. It is afternoon and while the music of the carnival is heard in the distance, the costume hangs in the doorway and rustles a little now and then in a breeze that I can't even feel on my sweaty body and bathing trunks. I've chosen a black Don Juan —tight black pants, a black shirt with wide arms and lace cuffs, a loose black cape, a black hat with light lace trim and a couple of tall nodding feathers. And, finally, the indispensable sword for duels.

Placed in its sheath, it restricts my movement. Dancing wouldn't be easy, wearing it, but who says that I'm going to be dancing this evening? I've disguised myself for the pleasure of disguising myself and don't have to throw myself into any carnival. Instead I'll probably put on my costume once more and enjoy it in front of the mirror before I go to bed and try to escape from the noise in sleep. I'll also use some time to put on my mask. I bought pancake makeup and mascara in the local drugstore and blue shadow for my eyelids (almost insurmountable language difficulties) and rouge to draw out my mouth and make it fuller. Powder, an eyebrow pencil, cold cream for afterward, and cotton. People make quite a production out of their disguises here, and I'm doing the same.

The music comes from small parades which are approaching the city, where they end by blending in an enormous witches' caldron. The local fantasy as far as costuming goes is completely free. There are no prototypes, or if there are, I don't know them. The favorite costume is that of a corpse: a black suit with a skeleton painted on it (possibly luminescent) and a primitive death mask. It is the children especially who enjoy playing corpse. But, on the whole, people use masks a lot—rather than makeup—and I have a feeling that many of the masks represent religious figures or historical personages. The parade does not walk or march, it dances, and it includes small musical instruments which it uses to emphasize the rhythm of the little orchestra that goes ahead of it. Tambourines, homemade flutes that can play only a couple of notes, guitars, and an occasional trumpet or clarinet.

The men go in front, the women after them. They haven't disguised themselves—they have simply dressed in gaily colored silk clothes and then added a half-mask to make themselves a little unrecognizable, anyway. Only a few women are wearing real masks or corpse costumes. They move easily in time to the rhythm while they make small cries like birds, and it isn't difficult to understand that they will continue dancing and moving until the carnival is over without becoming tired because you can see that they use hardly any energy —they are born to dance, and you wouldn't think they had a worry in their lives. But my Scandinavian conscience reminds me that they are living on the border of starvation, and now, on top of it all, they're not supposed to eat meat for . . . how long is it, eight weeks? They say goodbye to it without a worry.

Well, I guess I can't put off Bang any longer. Straus' review was torn out of the typewriter. I haven't got a grip on him yet and begin to doubt whether I ever will. Gave up making the review a little parody of style, but that means he writes about the same way I do, and that wasn't the intention either. The intention was to characterize the man as the perfect tactician. Here I am tearing a colleague to pieces, but I demand applause and bouquets because just see how honest I am. Give it to you straight, and for precisely that reason avoid taking a punch on the jaw because I am so damn honest. Aside from that, Straus *is* honest: he says what he believes. The main purpose of the review (in the development of the novel) is, naturally, to hurt Bang deeply. Straus has, it is true—still without dissembling —recommended the book; but, shrewd as he is, he has seen Bang's soft spot (one of them, a couple of them) and poured a lot of salt— Now I'm mixing metaphors again. In the novel's final form, Straus' review will naturally be combined with Bang's reactions. He sits on the edge of the bed, becomes more and more wide awake, perhaps gets another beer and begins to smoke. Or he turns off the radio and turns it on again, like the self-torturer he is. I'm a little bored with the thought of having to write it because Straus' review is the main thing and these interruptions with Bang's different reactions only slow it down and are simply all too predictable. Purely typographically, it is also unattractive; Straus' review has to be set in italics.

Aside from that, Straus as a character won't really hold together; the different models point each in its own direction. The owner of a country estate who goes hunting, the crime writer with even greater success than Bang, the street urchin who isn't afraid to say "balls" on the radio, the astute analyst (I have tried as much as I can to make him astute) who is taken seriously in *Vindrosen* and who, by using a little of his developed role-consciousness, could himself have a review accepted there. Role-consciousness is a good term because the intention was (is) that Straus is a superman who plays all roles equally well and possesses an extraordinary ability to size up situations. But can one get anyone to believe that all these roles lie hidden in the same man? I am also determined to be fair; caricature is easy for me and I have had to hold myself back in order to keep it between the lines. Straus is ridiculous "between the lines" because he lives on a country estate and attacks the bourgeois society, but on precisely that point I am perhaps so malicious that it appears to be an act of revenge, even though I keep it "between the lines" and don't comment on it. Straus is not easy to get a grip on—but back to Bang.

The radio program had scarcely ended (Bang is sitting on the edge of the bed; he is sitting on an electric heating pad because he has a poor back; on the table there is a beer and he has lighted a cheroot or cigar) before the telephone rang. Someone had heard the review and was extremely indignant for his sake. In the background the noise of a party—in other words, there are a lot of people who have heard it.

—God, what a perfidious fellow he is, and then all the time playing on how infernally honest he is. What a *little* man he is! I hope you . . . You heard it, didn't you?

—Yes.

—I hope you're above taking that man seriously. Had you gone to bed?

—Yes. I have a lot to do tomorrow.

—There are some of us sitting over here having a little party. You wouldn't want to come over and get a little moral support?

—Thanks, but I think I'd rather go to sleep now.

—If you should change your mind, we're here at my house. I'm to say hello for the others and to say that Straus is a stupid ox. You haven't thought about answering, have you?

—Naturally not.

—I see. Well, I guess you'd better go to sleep. Tomorrow there won't be a soul who'll remember that review.

Bang lay down and turned off the heating pad. As sometimes happened, the heat had made the pain in the small of his back (shooting all the way up into his neck muscles) stronger. He finished his beer, went to brush his teeth once more, moved the ashtray into the hall, and lay down again. After a few minutes he turned out the light and lay for a while on his back. Then he lay on his right side, the side he slept on, and tried to fall asleep.

The poet was right: I am a behaviorist. Now there should be something about what Bang thought, but there are only things about what he is doing. Theoretically, I should be able to write very good film scripts. A series of montages which show the sleepless Bang in different positions in the bed. He curls himself into a ball, stretches out. He turns the quilt over in order to get the cool side toward his body, throws it off altogether. Turns the light on and off, perhaps gets another beer, tries to read. Can't one guess what Bang is thinking? I simply am not able to describe it.

At one point Bang tries to tire himself out by reading, but the words blur on the paper in front of him. He went into the living room to get *In the Same Boat* and find the place that Straus had quoted in order to see if it was as bad as it had sounded. But he didn't have the courage to read his own book and it lay unopened on the night table. He had come to the feared point in time where the effect of Noludar was on a downswing and made him more and more wide awake, even agitated. Finally he went out to the kitchen, plugged in the coffee maker, and started to get dressed. He was aware that he couldn't drive now and ordered a taxi. At one o'clock (I call attention to the second line in the novel: *his* day) he drove toward the city to see people.

A new parade is going by on the road behind the hotels. The music reaches me and distracts me. It is late afternoon and the sun streams in between two palm trees and paints my hands red. How is it Kinbote's "preface" to *Pale Fire* goes—I quote by memory, but it is certainly very close: "There is a very loud amusement park in front of my present lodgings." I don't think I will get any further today. (I am quite aware of the fact that I am writing less every day, but I don't use less time—it just goes more slowly because it's going uphill; I am coming to the most difficult part, and it casts long deep shadows in front of it.)

The Don Juan costume is hanging in the doorway and sways in the light (that was the kind of word Straus picked on) evening breeze. I'll go into the city and take a look at the festivities. Later I'll get dressed and make myself up. I'm not sure that I'll go to the dance at the hotel; I don't know anyone here and don't want to know anyone, but I will make myself elegant and unrecognizable—that will be fun.

Once in a while things fall together. Bang is also on his way to a party.

February Twenty-third

Find myself still in a happy high from the champagne (what else should Don Juan drink?) and feel, though far from rested, the need to communicate with my I.B.M. It is some time in the morning; I am sitting in the shade, for a change, and am pleasantly chilly. Am whistling the Champagne Aria (reduced tempo, as well as I remember it) while I wait for the coffee percolator to start percolating.

Went to the ball after having been in the city during the afternoon and watched the parades and bought a half-mask (as if there were a risk of anyone recognizing me, but just wait). Went to the ball after a thorough limbering-up routine and a protracted makeup job. And in no time at all found myself in the company of the loveliest black girl.

There are certain things my typewriter can't do; among other things, it can't strike two keys at the same time, and that saves me the job I used to have of picking apart a whole swarm of keys when I tried to write fast once I really got going on something good. This one can't do that, but, on the other hand, it hits wrong keys and whole wrong words, and I guess I can't convince it to describe my little black girl in the manner she deserves. The impressions are fragmentary and somewhat conventional: large lips, white teeth, she dances with her stomach—I'm determined to stay away from olfactory impressions— her voice suddenly reminded me of my parents' old Josephine Baker records. We talked a mixture of English and French. Not the formidable Donna Anna, the pitiable Donna Elvira, nor the confused little Zerlina, but a girl who for some reason or other had decided that it might as well be me for this evening. Said she had seen me on the beach and in the lobby and that I acted as if I was hiding. Answered that I worked—except for this one evening. What kind of work? That was a secret. All right, but she had heard my typewriter.

I've taken care of my sex life (it hasn't been urgent) by hand power in the bathroom, or let come whatever wanted to come during the night, but now I felt like having a real screw, and the desire was clearly mutual. We went back to my bungalow with a bottle of champagne, found some music on my transistor radio, and shared the bottle in more and more relaxed positions on the edge of the bed. Unfortunately, there was something else that remained conspicuously relaxed, even after I had got her dress off (with her help—the mechanics of it were very complicated). We kept our half-masks on—hadn't exchanged names either. I don't know what she was supposed to represent in her silver dress. Here I guess one's carnival costume doesn't necessarily represent anything unless it represents death, and hers didn't do that.

Anyway, I couldn't get His Nibs to stand up—whether due to the champagne or to all the strange pills I devour. It didn't seem to worry the lady, and when I had given it all the chances it deserved, I decided to see that she at least got a little pleasure out of it, and went seriously to work with my green fingers and later with my tongue. She had perfumed (now I can't help it after all) her crotch and furthermore tasted of salt. My systematic work brought her to a point where, in the midst of my intoxication, I was very worried about her because of the degree to which she'd lost control of her breathing and lay there throwing herself from side to side. It began streaming out of her onto her groin and my fingers were one sticky mass, and, like some schoolboy, I began to wonder who would eventually change the sheets. Then came the payoff, for when she had got what she could reasonably expect and I had stopped making any demand whatsoever upon His Nibs, he at last began to stir, and she was kind enough to notice and

76

do something about it. Now the problem was to draw things out a bit, and she cooperated in that too, letting me slip out every time His Nibs was about to come. One time things were just about to go wrong, when she had him way down in her throat (that can't really have been the case, but that's how it felt) and I was afraid of choking her because she was obviously about to come again herself and one hears such awful stories, but I hurriedly began to think about a lot of other things and got him out again before he went off. She had found her way surprisingly quickly and without my help to my really sensitive spot, my right ear (I've never understood why the left one doesn't have the same magical lines of communication) and licked it hot with her rough little tongue. Came a moment later in the right place, just a single trip, but it was long and good and His Nibs still stayed hard enough so I could keep thrusting in the rhythm we had mutually agreed on quite a while after I'd emptied myself. Still in her but beginning to get limp, I reached for the champagne, and we took turns drinking out of the champagne bottle, and it didn't seem to bother her at all that I lit up a large cigar before our bodies separated so that she got a lot of smoke in her face. While I smoked, she started on my ear again, and I could feel His Nibs attempting to stir once more. But one shouldn't follow up a hard-won success, and I was well aware that with all the medicine and champagne the chances were pretty poor.

We ordered another bottle and went swimming together. Amusingly enough, she insisted on wearing my bathrobe to cross the beach, although there wasn't a soul in sight. Back in the room the new bottle stood in its ice bucket, and she got permission to taste my cigar and started to cough. There hadn't been much conversation, but suddenly she said in English, That accent of yours couldn't fool me anywhere, you're Danish, aren't you? Swedish, I answered. No, Danish, I lived with a Danish film producer three years. I kept on insisting I was Swedish while I racked my brain trying to think of a Danish film producer who had lived with a black girl for three years. Luckily, we had kept our half-masks on. I was really afraid for a moment, and it didn't help at all when she repeated that she could certainly hear the difference between a Swedish accent and a Danish one. You're a writer, aren't you? she asked, and I replied that I was a journalist. Got her to change the subject, but she came back several times to the point that she could definitely recognize a Danish accent when she heard one. When we had emptied the bottle, I accompanied her to her own bungalow, where she gave me a little kiss on my right ear and said that I would be permitted to keep my secrets to myself.

I've slept a little. I'm not sober yet, but I don't have a hangover and shall venture to approach good old Bang, who was also going to a party. The sun has risen while I've been writing, and my bungalow casts a long shadow across the terrace where I sit working. Now comes the really hard part, but I'm not afraid.

As was his custom, Bang got into the front seat next to the taxi driver and started a conversation in order to wake up more. One day you'll get around to writing a novel about a taxi driver, so it's a good thing to know something about the job. How does the taxi meter work? Can you disconnect it and cheat the company and the tax collectors? Who owns the car? How many hours a day does one drive? How much are the gross earnings, and how much the net? Are records kept of the trips? How much can you earn on a good day? Is it more fun to drive at night or during the day? The taxi was the same make of automobile as Bang's, but with a diesel engine and without automatic gears. Why not pay the additional price for these extras on a car when you have to drive over sixty thousand miles a year? Bang asked questions automatically, and let the answers go in one ear and out the other. His thoughts were on Straus—was he sitting up at his estate now, having just listened to himself on the radio? Or had he got to the point where he didn't listen to himself on the radio any more? Was he like Bang in that he couldn't stand to hear his own voice? It was half past one (check the earlier chapter) and the odds were that Straus was asleep and dreaming. What was he dreaming about? Did he also feed his subconscious before he went to bed? Did he also suffer from insomnia and have to bomb himself out with alcohol or sleeping pills? Bang had run out of questions, and the taxi driver grumbled about Lyngby Highway, which had been under construction for years. In Germany they complete such things in a month, he said.

Bang rounded off the fare shown on the taxi meter in the taxi driver's favor and tottered up the stairs on his rubber legs. There was a tremendous racket coming from the apartment, but no one opened the door when he rang the bell. Finally he took hold of the door handle and found he could just walk in. One of the living-room walls had been cleared of all pictures and was now filled with an orgy of color. Bang happened to get between the light-show apparatus and the wall and saw his shadow against the colored wall for a moment before people started shouting and made him duck down. Someone behind the light-show apparatus was dropping color from an eyedropper down between the two glass plates. The picture on the wall was reversed laterally so that the colors streamed upward, warmed by the heat, and blended together in gliding patterns. Someone recognized Bang and found him a seat by the apparatus and he had a glass stuck in his hand. A little later an aluminum-foil pipe was passed by, and he took a few drags before he let it go farther.

The host caught sight of Bang and sat down beside him. Pretty down? he asked. Bang shook his head. I wouldn't be either, if I were you. Some of us here heard the man, and, Christ, was he small. So successful and still he can't bear that someone else just comes *near* him. If you want to know what I think, he's got a lot of troubles of his own, otherwise a person doesn't act like that. Is there anything personal between you two?

—Not that I know of.

—What really makes me sick is this tremendous honesty. The way he covers himself so it actually becomes something really fine for him to strike a blow at his most dangerous competitor. Phew, it stank to high heaven! We're all agreed that it just simply stank.

The music being played for the light show was a high monotone beat music—the type Bang couldn't make head or tail of—and it was hard for him to hear what his host was saying. More people joined them, sat on the floor, and backed up the host's assertions. At one point the eyedropper and the paint tubes were foisted upon Bang. The others had tried to make patterns on the wall in dark intense colors; he wanted to try something in more pastel shades, but the glass in front of the light-show apparatus had got so turbid he couldn't do it, and he sat down by the apparatus again. He had asked for some softer music to accompany his patterns, but apparently there was only hard monotone soul music, or whatever it was, in the apartment. He got a refill in his glass, but let the pipe go by when it was offered to him again.

The conversation still centered on Straus' review. If you want to know what I think, it sounded more like an act of personal revenge than a review. The man practically intimated that you were impotent; anyway, that's the way it sounded to me. Have you considered giving an answer?

—What would I answer?

—Tell me, wasn't Nadja down at his country estate to do a personality feature on him?

—Yes, as script girl.

—Could there be something there? I mean, could she have stepped on his toes somehow? He is, you know, insanely thin-skinned where it concerns himself.

—I can't imagine it could be anything like that. She was only a script girl, after all.

—It's a case of unadulterated jealousy. No one above, no one on the same level, and no one below either—not that I think you're the least bit below him; the two of you are only different. You create the best plots and he writes better. I hope you don't mind my saying so?

The picture on the wall was dominated once again by dark colors which streamed upward before they blended together, flowed out in long tongues, and at last broke loose and formed small independent islands. Now and then the heat from the apparatus made one of the small islands explode, spread out, and form spiderweb patterns. Bang let his glass be refilled when a bottle was passed and let the others talk. It struck him that even here, where the sympathy was on his side, it was always Straus—Straus the mystery—that people talked about. They say he has two books on the way this year, someone said. Bang didn't tell them that there were three. Besides the television series for this summer, added somebody else. Someone mentioned a film script

Straus had written in one week in the Bahamas. The host had heard that Straus was preparing a book on elephant hunting that would be published with color plates—the photographs had been taken by Straus himself—in Czechoslovakia and printed in seven languages concurrently. Red color streamed up over the wall and by some sort of chemical process filled in all the gaps in the meshes of the black spiderweb. A little later the tape ran out, and the lights were turned on in the room so the host could put on some new music. When Bang struggled to his feet and turned around, there stood Nadja right behind him.

February Twenty-fourth

Blessed, blessed, each soul that has peace! Still no one knows the day before the sun goes down. Bang meets Nadja, the sun has gone down, but I don't have peace. I'm wide awake; the rhythm of my days has become hopelessly muddled. Have used most of the day to water down my champagne hangover with whatever I had on hand to drink in order to get slept out before this had to be written, but have only become more and more wide awake and more and more tired. Now it's midnight, and my typewriter stands humming, demanding that I write on it. Bang meets Nadja. His day (which I had originally planned for one chapter!) is about to end, and he doesn't know it yet. But I know it and now comes (I have said this a few times before) the most difficult part.

Met late this afternoon my black girl from last night. It was on the beach, and we talked a little as if I had only squired her around a bit for the evening. When she was going to leave, she said that the only thing she didn't understand was that I pretended to be a Swede. Asked her to look me up in the hotel register, and she answered that she had, in fact, done that. Before I had time to react, she laid a brown hand on my shoulder and said that I had the right to travel incognito; she liked small mysteries.

Bang meets Nadja, but I'm putting it off a little. Still unable to sleep and still not sober, I went to town late this afternoon. I had happened to think of our weapon collection at Baunebakke. Think somebody left a gallery rifle there last summer, but I'm not sure. Otherwise we only have air rifles. Here they require just as few documents for a weapon as for one of their hopeless sleeping remedies (also bought a few new samples of them), and I got a little pistol, more or less what you call a lady's pistol, I think, just to have in my pocket. As a lieutenant in the reserves, my brother had a pistol once. He took very good care of it and hid it carefully in the bottom of the white cupboard. I got permission to try it a couple of times, but I wasn't very good with it. Remember that it was thrown away ceremoniously by my parents after the accident, as if that made any difference then. He was a good shot. He took pains a couple of times to try to teach me the art.

There's a globe in the hotel lobby. I let it twirl around and found a little green Denmark where Fyn was placed too high up where Samsø Island should be. Traced with my finger from Copenhagen to Elsinore, which was not marked, and farther up and down along the coastline to where Tisvildeleje and the woods should have been. Would like to have a map of the woods in which to take imaginary walks, but I have to take them without the help of a map. Down the coastline to Brantebjerg, but then my brother pops up in front of me, and suddenly I have a gun in my hand, and I shoot without wanting to, and he crumples up, and blood spreads out in the snow like red ink (Straus can't stand metaphors) on a piece of blotting paper. Spanned the distance from North Zealand to here with my hand, but my hand was too small, my fingers wouldn't make it.

Had a conversation with the porter about one thing and another. There are no limits to what one can get for money here, but he sized me up—I did have circles under my eyes after so many hours without sleep, I'm sure. Gave him a couple of photographs I'd had taken in town with my new beard, and he promised to do what he could. I've no desire to meet my little black girl again; Denmark is small, and she insisted to the very end that she could hear the difference between a

Danish accent and a Swedish one. Was also dumb enough to take off immediately when she suggested that I say a few words in Swedish.

Someone had invited Bang and someone else had invited Nadja, or else she had come without an invitation. They hadn't seen each other since she had come to pick up the last of her things; two lawyers had taken care of the final arrangements. He knew that she had lived with a male friend for a while and believes she lives alone now. It is a little difficult for him to remain steady on his legs, and he burns his hand when he makes a grab for the hot light-show apparatus, which is about to tip over.

They say hello to each other and she says she heard Straus. It wasn't fair, she says; you know I thought it was a good book (she had read it in rough draft). He nods and asks how is she and she answers that she is fine. He is fine too. She takes a sip from her glass and asks if he is working on a new book. He nods. The one with the salesman? He admits that and tries to remember what it was Straus said about him . . . that he sniffed women instead of smelling them. There is a strong scent of Chamade about her, and there aren't many who use it; it is her scent, and it still makes his head swim.

I must try to get Nadja into focus. This is just an informal get-together, and she hasn't dressed up. She is wearing black velveteen pants, and she has a black sweater on. I'm too disoriented to remember how I've described her before and give up all attempts to fool the enemy. Have, I'm sure, told about the gold fillings in her back teeth that are visible when she smiles. She is warm and smells (can't help it) as if she has just got out of an unscented bath. Now I'm contradicting myself, but scents are something that are added; there is a warm smell of her herself, her own clean sweat in her clothes. I didn't get finished with her clothes—she has on a short-sleeved black sweater. Hope this agrees with what I have written before, but she has black hair and green eyes. Now is the time one should look back and see what one has written, but I don't feel up to it: This is the real Nadja. Remember a phrase that she looks used, which makes one think that she can be used. I don't have to retract that. The scent—excuse me, the smell of her hits Bang (like a punch in the stomach, I was going to write, but that's because I'm so tired I can't find anything better) and he wants her back, while he looks for something he can support himself with in order to keep his balance.

Something has happened to the party. People realize that they have met each other and that nobody has planned it (or has someone planned it?). The room has grown quiet. The fellow with the tape-recorder rewinds hurriedly and finds some dance music, two men work frantically (excuse my adverbs, I've run out of inspiration) to change the glass plates and begin again with new colors. Nadja smiles so that he sees all her gold fillings and asks if they shouldn't dance together.

Each time I stop to think, the stillness is filled with the typewriter's impatient hum. I ought to go to bed, but I know that the bed will sail over the lobby's globe in the direction of that little green blob they have tried to make resemble Denmark. I must continue, cannot allow myself to take more of my colored pills. I have to stick to the bottle and later clean up my "style." I need some dialogue now.

The radio crackles on my table. I don't have the strength to find any music—here there's music all night long, and there are many programs to choose between. They dance, he holds his hands on her hips (I was going to write warm hips): the feel of her pelvis (is that where it is?) is pleasant through the thin protection of velveteen. Little by little he pulls her closer and closer to him. The party seems to loosen up (does Bang realize so much in his condition?); now and then they glide past the light-show apparatus and cast large shadows on the new pictures. They don't dance any closer than is necessary for them to talk.

—Do you still live alone? asks Nadja.

He nods. A little later:

—And you?

—Right now, yes.

—You got the place with the kitchenette?

—Yes. Do you still get around and see some people?

—Now and then. You know, I've just started on a book. I'm right at the point . . .

—Where it's very convenient for you to be alone.

—Yes and no. I miss you. (Hey, that's moving pretty fast.)

—And the translation? How's that going?

—I'll never get that finished—that book can't be translated.

—I'm not surprised. You'd never get me to read it all the way through.

In a series of montages we see them dancing together. I'm the one who decides the speed and I have the whole night in front of me. My intuition is that this must not go too fast; my head is blown empty and my famous "small details" will not put in an appearance. He holds her closer (here also, Straus should have had something to say) and when he speaks, he speaks into her hair—no, she has brushed her hair behind her ears, and they are red, as if she has just got out of the bathtub—which she probably just has.

—You're not here with anybody tonight?

—No. That fellow Straus, is there anything personal between the two of you?

—Not that I know of.

—It seemed as if there was.

Montage, later:

—You went along for that interview with him. Did he know that we were married then?

—I don't think so. I was just the script girl, after all. He was fantastic. He always knew what he wanted to say: we never had to do any retakes.

The montages will later be replaced with details from the party. There is a pause in the music and they stand by the tape-recorder and have something to drink. When they are dancing again, he has to support himself against her.

—You're sure there isn't anything personal between you?

—Hey, are you drunk?

—A little.

But then she is too; she has drunk quite a bit in order to get into a party mood.

—One has to grant that he's honest, or at least not afraid of being taken to task. It would have been easier for him to praise you.

—Yes.

—How is *In the Same Boat* doing?

—Nicely. Excuse me.

The last was due to the fact that Bang is about to throw them both off balance, and she throws her arms around him. A tremendous desire to mount her again wells up in him. They kiss each other and dance in place, leaning on each other. The party is breaking up. Somebody has turned off the light-show apparatus (it is still dark outside; I've no idea what time it is; my watch is lying on the night table and I've no desire to go over and look at it).

—May I take you home? (This is going too fast, and I who usually have such a knack for parties.)

—In a little while.

Have been out to look at the night sky without turning off the typewriter. Bottle in hand. The constellations remind me of August nights at Baunebakke, but I can't find the Big Dipper and Orion. Doesn't one see them here? I found the Milky Way after having looked a little while, down low over my palm trees. Isn't it higher in the sky at home? I can't get the Milky Way and the palm trees into focus at the same time. In my room the typewriter is humming, waiting for me; I've forgotten to close the screen door, and mosquitoes are coming into my lighted room. I want to take a bath now, but my typewriter calls me back.

The party is thinning out. Bang stands leaning against the wall, and Nadja comes over to him with two filled glasses.

—Are you driving?

—Taxi.

—You can take me home now if you like. I hope you don't misunderstand the situation. (Would she talk like that? She's no schoolgirl, but she's had a lot to drink. Perhaps she's smoked too.)

To drive in a taxi through Copenhagen on a winter night. Frost-glistening streets, neon lights that burn all night long, waiting for a red light at an empty intersection. My typewriter will do many things, but it staggers each time I get homesick. I'm not sure I can write this thing to the end.

—Do you want to come up or do you want to go home? I can make up a bed for you.

—Come up.

An interminable suburban street in Copenhagen. She lets herself in and he follows her. He has to stop and catch his breath at each landing. She leads him into a living room with furniture and pictures he recognizes and disappears into the bedroom. I'm not sure that I can go on. She comes back with a glass of tomato juice. Disappears again and comes back this time with bedclothes to make up a bed on the sofa, the one that used to be in the guest room. The typewriter hums indefatigably; my bottle is empty.

She's also brought a glass of tomato juice for herself, and they sit side by side and drink. He puts his arm around her shoulder and she leans toward him. He kisses her and his tongue runs over her gold fillings. His hand finds (remember Straus' warnings) its way to that place where the short sweater separates itself from the slacks and feels its way up over her back; she doesn't have anything on under this sweater, but presses her arms in toward her body so that he has to be content with her back. With his unoccupied hand he strokes her neck and shoulders the way he knows she loves to have it done. His hand glides down along her back, down to the waistband of her slacks, in under it, finds the crevice.

She holds him out at arm's length and looks at him, smiling.

—Would you rather sleep with me in my bed?

—Yes, thank you.

—Fine. But just for tonight. I'd like to, too, but you mustn't misunderstand. We're not going to start all over again—it's finished (overtones of unreadable novels) between us. Are we agreed?

—Agreed.

He succeeds in getting her sweater off; she helps him unbutton his shirt. He lies back in the rolled-up bedclothes and pulls up his undershirt while her hand feels its way down under the waistband of his trousers, in under the tight waistband, and begins to caress him (where? Straus would be precise). Contrary to expectation, there is no reaction.

Called a bleary-eyed porter for a new bottle. Ignore the typing mistakes and have stopped x-ing out the wrong words. Am drinking from my toothbrush mug and thinning with tap water (forgot to order a siphon and ice and don't have the heart to ring again). Fade down, fade up. We are in her bedroom. She has bought a new wide bed.

—Wouldn't it be better if we just go to sleep?

He shakes his head, and she patiently does everything that she usually does, everything that usually works.

—I don't think it wants to tonight.

—Yes it does.

—The trouble with you is that you want to do more than you can. You didn't have (she's also drunk) particularly good endurance as a lover, but that wasn't why I left you. You weren't particularly imaginative either, but I don't think that matters so much. What was wrong with you was that you were never satisfied with yourself. You wanted to do more than you could. Things were never completely good enough (check with description in ch. ?). You always want to do more than you can, you always destroy the enjoyment for yourself because you want to do more than you can.

How did Bang become the way he was? Should I have described his childhood and found a short ingenious explanation there? Should we have heard about his dreams? (The behaviorist short-cut?) Is he a victim of society, or was he born the way he is? That can perhaps be dealt with, but it won't be tonight (I sense a faint gray light over the veranda; the stars are beginning to get faint).

—Can't we just lie together and be good to each other? Do you absolutely have to perform now? It doesn't *want to* tonight.

—Nadja, I want you back again.

—You can't have that. I thought we understood each other. And now I can't do any more. I want to sleep.

Nevertheless, he got her to try just a little more, half sleeping and with closed eyes.

—Him, the other one—he didn't want to do more than he could, did he?

—No.

—Was it Straus?

—Straus? Are you mad?

—Have you told him I was impotent?

—You're not impotent, you're just—oh, stop it.

Perhaps I can write this to the end, but it won't help me sleep. He has put his hands around her neck.

—Was it Straus?

—Let me go. I want to sleep.

—Have you talked to him about me?

She tried to take his hands away, and he tightened his grip.

—You have talked to him about me?

She didn't answer, but tried to get his hands away. She tried to twist herself loose, and he clamped his legs around her knees. Suddenly she stopped fighting him and lay there with wide-open eyes. I kept on pressing my hands against her throat even though I knew she was dead.

March

March Fourth

Mr. Anthony Baxter leans forward and looks at the sun for the last time before the airplane descends through the cloud cover. The little FASTEN SEATBELTS sign goes on, but he has already done that. He looks with a smile at his seatmate, who discreetly crosses himself. Then he takes his papers out of his inside coat pocket: his baggage claim checks, his traveler's checks, his passport. He opens his passport to the page with the photograph and looks at it, smiling, while he thinks about a helpful porter and numerous other helpful people and about a place where formalities such as prescriptions for medicine or a permit to buy a revolver are not necessary.

While the plane descends through the cloud cover, he takes off his dark glasses and polishes them. While he has his pocket handkerchief out he rubs his eyes—but cautiously, because he still feels as though he might press the contact lenses against his eyeballs and perhaps dislodge or lose them. His eyes are always watering, and it is especially bad this morning as the plane prepares to land after the long sleepless flight.

Anthony Baxter has had a few drinks along the way, but he has restrained himself, and he has given up taking any sleeping pills because he knows that they will only make him more wide awake. There were Danish newspapers aboard the plane, and he has used the long flight to read them from front to back. Therefore it comes as no surprise to him when the plane finally drops below the cloud cover and he sees the ice beneath him. He presses his nose against the window. The airplane is clearly about to make a turn; it goes out over land—that must be Skaane, that must be Malmø right under him. There are channels in the Øre Sound, but the Sound is frozen over and there are ships that look as if they are frozen in. Even though the weather is cloudy, the plane casts a small cross on the ice. They are much too high up to prepare for a landing, and glide next over Saltholm and a little later in over Copenhagen a good distance north of Kastrup Airport. Someone behind Baxter wants to see out the window, but he sprawls in front of the entire window and doesn't move. Copenhagen is more gray than white, but the lakes are white, and when the plane banks, Tivoli comes into view, and the deserted Tivoli is also white. One can see the tower of the City Hall and one can guess which is the Politiken Building on the opposite corner. The S.A.S. Building towers up out of the gray city, and the Codan Building and the new silo at Carlsberg Breweries. Then comes the Damshus Lake, which is also white, and then the airplane banks again and goes into a gentle turn over a series of gray suburbs. Baxter lets the man behind him lean forward to look out of the window for a moment, but then pushes him back somewhat roughly, for he's caught sight of a highway and something that can't be anything but Mill Creek, and a moment later there's a bridge over the highway with heavy traffic going into the city, and that can't be anything but the bridge at Nærum, and now Baxter can clearly see the shopping center and the church and the town pond, and beyond the town is a little handful of gray row houses with snow in their yards. Then they fly out over the woods and toward the Øre Sound again, and straight across the airplane, through a window on the opposite side, Baxter catches a glimpse of Hermitage Plain and Hermitage Castle before they are out over the frozen Sound again.

They fly directly south of Hven, in over Sweden again, and now they are dropping down fast with small poppings in the ears that make you nearly deaf. At low altitude the plane flies over Saltholm for a second time and comes down for a landing at Kastrup. The man next to him crosses himself again discreetly, and then comes the first little bump, followed by a couple of still smaller ones, and it sounds as if the engines are speeded up while the plane, braking violently, storms across the landing strip. Baxter has taken out a little mirror and studies his face while he alternately puts his glasses on, takes them off, and polishes them. His initials are stitched on his pocket handkerchief: A.B. At last he decides to put the glasses in their case and stick them in his pocket. He dries his eyes with his handkerchief and inspects himself once more. It seems to him that he appears nearsighted without glasses, which he has worn since he was a little boy, but thanks to the contact lenses he looks fine, or he would look fine if his eyes didn't keep on watering. The plane comes to a standstill, and a new little pop brings most of his hearing back. The plane taxis in to the terminal and is brought to a stop, and the FASTEN SEATBELTS sign goes off. Baxter takes his time; he is one of the last to step into the aisle and get his hand luggage and his overcoat down from the rack over the seats. He turns the large fur collar up tightly around his neck before leaving the plane with a portable typewriter in one hand and a light-weight suitcase and a fur hat in the other.

The passport inspector does not so much as look up to compare the passport photo with Baxter when Anthony Baxter, who in the meantime has put on his hat and pulled the two small flaps down over his ears, walks past. Baxter collects his suitcases from the conveyor belt and takes them on a little cart over to Customs. Here things don't go as smoothly—an inspector insists upon opening the suitcases and rummaging through them. There are summer clothes in the suitcases which are inappropriate for the Danish winter, but there's nothing on which he must pay duty. At the bottom of one of the suitcases is a blue folder containing a little pile of loose typewritten pages, but the inspector doesn't open that.

There is no one waiting for Baxter, and he wasn't expecting anyone either. In the transit hall he buys a morning paper and sticks it in the pocket of his coat without reading it. When he steps outside, it is bitter cold, and he stops and breathes deeply the frosty air, appearing remarkably relaxed before he hires a taxi. Whether because of Baxter's clothes or skin color or his foreign-looking suitcases, the taxi driver addresses Baxter in English when he has settled down in the front seat beside the driver. Baxter hasn't said anything—it seems as though he's been waiting for the other to ask.

—Where can I take you?

—Are you prepared for a long trip?

—It depends on how long, sir.

—I'm going to something called . . . wait a moment.

Baxter pulls a slip of paper out of his pocket and reads something on it.

—Do you know a place called . . . you'd better read it yourself.

The taxi driver reads what is on the paper.

—Tibirke Bakker. That's all right, sir. About an hour's drive.

They drive in toward the city. The snow is piled up in small dirty heaps along the side of the road, and the road is crowded with grimy cars. Baxter wipes his window, which has fogged up, and peers out curiously.

—Could we pass the Town Hall Square, please?

—Yes, sir.

—And could you put on a little more heat?

They pass the Raadhusplads and Baxter rolls down his window and glances up at the large billboard on the Politiken Building, which has an advertisement for that morning's edition of *Ekstrablad*. NEW TV SUCCESS FOR STRAUS, it says. He rolls the window down again and lights a Henry Clay cigar after having clipped it. After a few puffs he puts it down and asks the driver to stop at a tobacco store. He comes back with a pack of Danish cigars, which he slits open with his fingernail, lighting one up after having thrown the other cigar out the window. They drive north, and now they have the lane more or less to themselves; the heavy traffic is moving toward the city, their lights slicing the cold foggy air.

—I can see you've been where the sun is shining, the driver says.

Baxter nods without answering. They pass Storkereden and Mill Creek and drive up toward the Nærum shopping center.

—Would you mind turning right here? I know it's out of the way, but I'd just like to have a look at something.

A little perplexed, the taxi driver turns and drives through the city according to Baxter's directions. First up to the shopping center, back to the main street again, and then down past the candle factory, past the church, and out along Rundforbi Road a little way. Baxter has rolled the window down again and glances up at the gray row houses. Halfway down the road, Baxter asks the driver to stop and turn around; Baxter looks up at a house with blue window frames standing behind a little yard with a large larch tree. They drive back, past the church and the town pond and the children's home, and up to the highway again, where they continue north.

In Helsinge, Baxter asks the driver to stop again, and he comes back to the taxi carrying several shopping bags. They continue north, and Baxter observes the snow-covered landscape.

—You like your car? Baxter asks.

—I like it very much.

—I used to drive a Mercedes myself. Do you know where I can hire a Mercedes?

—You should have tried in Copenhagen.

—I suppose so.

From the top of a hill there is a view of Tibirke Bakker and the snow-clad woods behind the hills. They turn left at Klint's Grocery. Baxter has long since started on a new cigar.

He gets the driver to stop by the village school and takes out his wallet. The taxi driver offers to drive all the way up into the hills, but Baxter explains that the nose-heavy taxi would get stuck and that he doesn't have far to go anyway. The driver wants to help with his suitcases, but Baxter refuses the offer and hoists up his suitcases and typewriter and shopping bags himself after he sees the taxi disappear.

It's almost impossible for him to hold on to all of the things, and he slips several times. He studies the tracks in the snow carefully— at first there are many, but the farther up the hill he goes, the fewer there are. After Essmann's farm there are only animal tracks in the snow, and Baxter stops, completely exhausted, and looks back. Below lies Arre Lake covered with ice. He puts all his things down while he waits to catch his breath again. Then he picks up everything and walks back a short distance. Stops again and looks around, listens. Finally he walks off the side of the road and up toward the woods again, jumps across a little ditch, and continues on between the first trees, where his all-too-thin shoes sink deep into the snow.

Once or twice he falls, but quickly gets up again, brushes the snow off himself, and stuffs various packages and cans which have fallen out of the shopping bags into them again. After a while he catches sight of the first house, a dark-stained pine house with orange shutters that shine between the trees. His eyes are watering in the intense cold, and he stands blinking a little before he goes on.

He approaches the houses cautiously and studies the snow, but there are still only animal tracks. He sets his things down among some trees and stealthily creeps right up to the house. The shutters are closed and there is no sign of life. He goes around behind the kitchen, finds the key on the ladder, and a moment later has let himself into the house.

The room smells of wood stain and wood and burned logs. Just inside the door, under the key rack, stands a vase of dried flowers. He crosses the room and taps the barometer while continuing to listen for sounds that might be approaching. But there is no sound other than the sighing of the woods and once in a while a car way down on the road. The barometer stands at SEHR SCHÖN; when he taps it, it drops a little.

There are birch logs and a can of kerosene by the fireplace, and he makes a fire before he goes back to pick up his things. He puts the shopping bags in the kitchen, connects the bottled gas, lifts two water buckets onto a shoulder yoke and goes down to the well for water. Later he sits in front of the fireplace with a mug of coffee and the day's fourth cigar. His suitcases are on the floor behind him and the typewriter is on the table between the two kerosene lamps.

Perhaps one should always write in the present tense—it's a comfortable form that doesn't lure you into stylistic capers. The writing goes post-haste. The keys on my little typewriter get all tangled up, so I have to untangle them all the time, getting ink on my fingertips. Sometime I'd like to write a novel entirely in the present tense—on the whole, I'm full of plans. Straus once wrote a novel in diary form. I'd like to try that too. I think it would be easy. Of course, it was the writer of the diary himself who had committed the murder. You write as much or as little as you want to every day—no fuss about chapters or composition. If you write badly one day, then it's because the diarist writes badly—you can turn it to a stylistic advantage. The novel was, as a matter of fact, far too well written. The diarist wrote just like Straus himself, and he's incapable of writing really badly. (Even though I believe he could write much better if he did some rewriting as I do, instead of just turning in his rough drafts to the publisher. But now I'm going to be nice to Straus.)

Baxter fascinates me. Too bad that I have to let him go. I think he's already proved worthy of a leading role. Something about the style, this jumping right into the middle of an action, reminds me of *Everything You Want,* my greatest success, which I wrote in three euphoric summer weeks (aside from the chapter in Tangiers, where I had to go to research it first and got depressed because Nana didn't send a single letter or even a postcard). I'm a little unclear about it now, but I'm afraid that Anthony Baxter's story will turn out to be a bit too close to that of Scherfig's "missing administrator." The missing author? I suppose I should have let myself be blown up on Amager Common (if I remember correctly), but unfortunately there wasn't time for that. But they haven't looked for me here in weeks, and that's a good sign. No one thinks a person is crazy enough to take refuge so close by. But I have to be careful.

Away with Bendix, Bang, and Baxter. I take leave of all my main characters and projects and sit back with a typewriter that at least doesn't declare its impatience by a steady delicate hum. What now? For whom am I writing now? Travel fatigue and the time difference make me confused, and I won't write any more. I think I can sleep now, but I'm full of ideas, and I can feel a large fantastic novel taking shape in me.

I'm cold, and the contact lenses make my eyes water, so I can't see the keys of the typewriter very well even though I've lit both the kerosene lamps. The most important thing is that I am home again. I am home in Denmark.

March Sixth

Mr. Klint, the grocer, will be the crucial test. Or rather Mrs. Klint, because she's the one who has the sharp eyes. I have my good reasons for putting off the test for a little while, but sooner or later it must be faced. If they recognize me, then everyone will recognize me; I've done business there for eight years, and if I can't fool them, there are too many others I can't fool. But for the time being I'm shopping at a grocer's halfway into town where they don't know me, because there is something that must be arranged first and that takes up my time pretty well. If they recognize me at Klint's, it will be necessary to get away in a hurry, and for that my legs alone won't do. It isn't enough that I'm carrying all my capital on me—I have to have my means of transportation right outside the door; therefore I've gone to the garage and got my old rusty Tiger Cub motorcycle out. It naturally wouldn't start even after I'd filled it with gas and fresh oil and pumped it up and tried to start it by pushing it in the snow. It needed a new battery, and yesterday I went down to get that along with new supplies— everything I forgot in Helsinge.

Snow has fallen two nights in a row and my tracks are quickly wiped out. Nevertheless, I now take the short-cut to the town through the woods and I have a couple of places where I jump over the ditch. At my present grocery and at the garage I speak English, and they answer as well as they can. I have my collar up around my ears, but sometimes I have the feeling that the whole thing can become too mysterious. Klint will be the big test and tomorrow that will occur, and the Tiger Cub will be ready.

I study myself in the mirror over the green washbasin. The hair and beard and tan do a lot, but a definite thing is the eyes. I'm very nearsighted and I've worn glasses since I was seven years old. Without the dark-rimmed glasses I seem to myself to be someone else. My eyes are larger, and the same is true of the area around my eyes, and even the color of my eyes is changed—I am red-eyed because the contact lenses still bother me, and I look nearsighted even though I look very nice when my eyes aren't running.

My English is good; I affect no accent in order not to seem unnecessarily mysterious. But in front of the mirror I practice pitching my voice lower. Nevertheless, I'm afraid of Mrs. Klint. She keeps good track of what's going on in Bakkerne, and she has plenty of time at this season of the year. I don't dare let her see my Tiger Cub because she would immediately recognize it; I have to make the last bit of the trip stealthily in neutral gear and hide the motorcycle around the corner, being sure that it will start with the first kick.

This afternoon the old monstrosity, which I never thought would function again, has run like a dream. I bought it with the advance from my first novel; later, when we got a car, I let this motorcycle stand far back in the garage and took it out each summer and polished it and drove it a few times out of loyalty. The motorcycle is fun in the hills, but it is not easy to control in loose snow. The tank is painted silver, the frame is black; it is a small easy machine which can be started by pushing it if the kick starter should conk out, but I don't dare take that risk. When it was new, I had a very personal relationship with it, such as I never had with my automobile: it was a living being, a little lively animal—a tiger cub precisely. I've taken many trips on it, some of them with Nana behind me, her hands clasped in front of me on my stomach. She was as fond of it as I was and was the perfect back-seat passenger who followed the machine in its slightest movements. One morning we drove right through the woods down to the beach and went swimming. I was very good at trail biking, but I had never tried it in snow. If they have been up here (and I can't imagine otherwise), it is very kind of them to have left the motorcycle. Have they already sold the house in Nærum? And who are they? We owned the house together; can her brother have been in action already? An unpleasant thought: have they also sold the house here, and am I taking the risk that one day the new owner will troop up here? I keep my ears open, the motorcycle stands ready right outside the house, and I don't take a step without having my money and my papers with me. It's an enormous risk I'm running; my only advantage is that I know my way around here.

I've gotten slept out after the time change and travel fatigue, and a final little pop in my ear has brought back my complete hearing again. I've sawed firewood for the stove and taken the portable phonograph into the living room. The most essential things I keep in a little red leather bag which is hanging by the door so I can get hold of it in a hurry. This evening I sat and played old Aksel Schiøtz: ah, I am at home/in the beloved land of my birth / With those I love / and who l-love me. It isn't only the contact lenses that make my eyes runny. I who write so hard-boiled.

When the living room is warmed up by the stove it smells exactly as it does in the summer. The phonograph has got stuck in the middle of a record because I forgot to wind it up, and out of the horn of the phonograph comes a gentle hum as if it picks up and transmits the soughing in the woods. I close the shutters when I light the oil lamp, and I stuff an old sweater into the phonograph horn to muffle the music, but I am afraid of the smoke which rises from the chimney and must be visible from far away. I'll have to get the gas heater working so I can manage without my beloved wood-burning stove, which lies smoldering after I've gone to bed in the alcove and have pulled the dividing curtain. I sleep with all my clothes on, partly to keep warm and partly so that I could leave in a hurry. Even when I'm sleeping I lie listening for an automobile crawling up toward the house in low gear, but I don't believe that you could get a car up here in all this snow. All the worse—that means they'll come on foot, and I'm not sure I can hear that. I should have chosen another house, a house near the west coast, but it was Baunebakke that I longed for.

Up in the bedroom I discovered to my surprise that some of Nana's summer clothes are hanging there. The scent of her perfume hit me in the face when I looked through the clothes. If they have been up here (and they have) they've left the clothes hanging here, and that suggests that they haven't tried to sell the house yet. Perhaps they're waiting until spring. There is much that I must find out.

Yesterday I went through the woods (a wide arc around the forest ranger's where we buy strawberries and potatoes in the summer) to get the battery and buy some things in town. Passed the bookstore and ventured in when I had made sure that only the assistant was in the store. Guess who they had in the window, albeit only in paperback. Bought the daily paper and H. C. Andersen's fairy tales. "Aunt Toothache" is called the same thing in Danish, and it strikes me as equally incomprehensible. Otherwise my reading is limited to what we have in the bookcase over the barometer: Bergsøe's *From Field and Forest,* old books on mushrooms, and Gelsted's book about the local district with Ib Andersen's drawings. Unpacked *Pale Fire* and made one of the usual hopeless attempts at continuing the translation. In the firewood box I found newspapers and weekly magazines from last summer and read about a visit at Straus' country estate, which I had skipped at the time. The yellowing newspapers were full of old news and pictures of people drinking beer in summer warmth and swimming without swimsuits down near Brantebjerg. The magazine showed the latest bathing apparel and gave recipes for easy summer food. I had to sacrifice them in order to get a fire going in the fireplace.

I must go to Helsinge and read the old newspapers. Was too busy that day and guess that it was several days before the news reached page one because of the way I handled things when I came to my senses again (telephoned the TV center and reported her sick). Strange how much presence of mind I mobilized in those days; something came out in me that I didn't know was in there—"With Your Back to the Wall," as my article said. I wonder where they're looking for me now, or if they've given up. The case must have given a real boost to my sales, but how am I going to find out about it? I've got more questions than answers.

In Nana's dresser I found quite a bit of makeup—among other things, an eyebrow pencil; I'll try that in front of the mirror. But I realize that there's also a risk I can be too mysterious-looking.

It's snowing outside, but it's still light. We are approaching the equinox, and the evenings are becoming longer. Tomorrow I will steer my little Tiger Cub down to Klint's and let things be put to the test. I don't know whether I want to stand face to face with Mrs. Klint. If she recognizes me, I don't have much chance. If it works, then I've won a respite.

March Seventh

Today's the day. After having warmed up to the cold trip with a little whiskey, I took my old Tiger Cub down to the edge of the woods and started it there. It's still snowing and my tracks are quickly covered. In a few minutes I was as familiar with the cycle's balance as if I had driven it just a few days ago. Loose snow is not bad to drive in; I prefer it to frozen tracks. I'd been unable to resist the temptation to really deck myself out: my fur hat down around my ears, my collar turned up around my neck, my eyebrows touched up with Nana's pencil, and as a last-minute inspiration (and here perhaps I went too far) a little rouge on both cheeks, as if the cold air didn't redden them enough. But I have my appetite back again by sawing wood and fixing up the motorcycle out in the fresh air, and I'm afraid my hollow cheeks are about to disappear.

The trial by fire began immediately, for Mrs. Klint stood at the counter. I walked around the store a little and got a chance to say something in English to her assistant while I filled my shopping basket. There's something to the idea that often you can recognize people by their physical bearing long before you see their faces or hear their voices, and I had used the previous day to rehearse a very distinctive way of walking. I bend a little at the knees and drag my legs, at the same time leaning forward slightly from the hip. It's very tiring, but I won't deny that it's also very amusing to try to carry it off. Well, I collected various things in my basket and dragged myself over to the counter, where Mrs. Klint sat enthroned. Resisted at the last moment an impulse to lay the day's newspaper on top of my purchases, and looked down at my wallet while I asked in English, "How much?"

I had the feeling I was being carefully examined while she rang up the purchases on the cash register—and I've undoubtedly given her something to think about—but if she recognized me, she didn't give any sign of it. I made quite a comic production of not being able to figure out the Danish money, which gave me a good excuse not to look up. Next time she'll have become used to me, and I'll risk looking straight into her curious eyes. She stared after me when I walked out of the store, and I'm sure she's got a story to tell, but I'm pretty sure it's not about me, because that she couldn't have kept hidden.

I walked back to my motorcycle, which I'd left out of sight at a suitable distance, and drove with my purchases in a shoulder bag (whiskey, cigarettes, a few canned goods) to Helsinge, where I dug up the old newspapers in the library. It had taken five days before anyone thought of gaining entrance to the apartment, but then my picture was on the front page next to hers—vanished without a trace, her separated husband, the last person she was seen with. The next day's paper still had the story on the front page, and by now they had, of course, discovered that most of my money had disappeared with me. WROTE ABOUT MURDER, IS NOW SUSPECTED OF MURDER HIMSELF—I'd already guessed that headline, but I hadn't guessed it would take them five days. I wouldn't have had to hurry so much.

The next day we were still on the front page, and a story boxed in a red frame disclosed that my books were really being snapped up. The reporter had telephoned Mogens Knudsen and asked if there were plans to bring out new editions, but he said there were no such plans. Nobody fell for my ruse of putting an empty bottle of sleeping pills on her night table, and it didn't help, either, that I had wiped off all my fingerprints. No, when one flees that way, he admits his guilt, and I was prepared for that. Jealousy as a motive behind the murder drama was the predictable theory, and guests who'd been at the party were questioned as to how much we had had to drink. Nothing was said about the fact that there was also smoking going on; after all, people know what they should tell the police. Nana got some nice compliments along the way—she was an excellent script girl, well liked by everyone. The library had only the morning papers, and I had to guess what the afternoon papers made out of the story.

The third day they had discovered that I had taken a charter flight to Tangiers, but there they lost track of me, and the fourth day the story moved to the inside pages, and there wasn't anything new in it, aside from the fact that my books were impossible to get either in the bookstores or at the libraries. Fromberg, you should have got an extra edition into the works while there was time!

I can still be somewhat amazed at my cold-bloodedness. That kind of person is hidden in me, too, but I could never have done it without my Valium pills. After my blackout, when I slept like a log on her sofa, I was never in doubt as to what I should do—the thought of turning myself in never crossed my mind. My theory proved correct —when your back is against the wall, the only thing that counts is the instinct for self-preservation. After a few days the story worked itself farther and farther back into the inside pages of the newspaper until at last it disappeared entirely. But I succeeded in getting more newspaper coverage in one week's time than Straus has ever had or probably will ever get, unless he takes it into his head to commit a murder, too. Rode the cycle back to Bakkerne, as far as the last stretch along the edge of the woods, and left it there while I crept stealthily up to the house. If Mrs. Klint had recognized me, they would be waiting for me now, but no one was there, and I dragged the cycle up to the house, all ready to go, right outside the door.

I used to talk with L. about the relationship between life and literature and was for once actually about to convince him of something. Of course, he didn't think you could replace the one with the other, but he had to concede at a later consultation that one could remedy much in himself by writing down his troubles and working off his aggressions. Was obviously on occasion not completely sure— I believe the word "sublimate" was right on the tip of his tongue, but he is a polite person and clearly could not bring himself to say that if I was to get any real relief I would have to write something more "refined" than crime novels. He reads all my books, considers it an obvious part of the therapy, but never comments on anything other than the details—he shrewdly finds the passages with which I have taken considerable pains. He's something of a mind-reader and soon guessed that I felt overshadowed by Straus. Don't think things are so much easier for Straus than they are for you, he said—you can see a mile away that he has his problems too. He made light of a suggestion that I stop writing (in any case, for a while). You know perfectly well you can't stop—you just shouldn't make believe you'll solve all your problems by writing. Amusingly enough, he often said so much the same thing as Nana (or the other way around) that you'd think they'd talked together behind my back. Nana also thought I should continue writing and try to stop competing with Straus and myself. Both of them were horrified by my fantasy of collaborating on a book with Straus—I would supply the plot and he would add the flesh and blood to it. L. compared the idea to animals that give up during a fight and turn over and expose their throats. Obviously believed that Straus wouldn't respect the rules and would bite hard. However, in other respects he isn't too bright, L.; he smokes forty cigarettes a day even though he has a bad heart, and he confided to me once when I asked for a new kind of sleeping pill that he had even more trouble sleeping than I did. What kind of hands do we put our fate into, anyway?

As a matter of fact, I wouldn't mind talking with him right now, but that would certainly be putting too much of a strain on his professional duty to remain silent. I wonder what he thinks about life and art now. Does he still think that I am sublimating? He was the one who wrote my prescriptions for Valium and Noludar—admittedly under strong pressure, because he doesn't believe in medicine; he thinks that you should cure yourself rather than suppress the symptoms, but he wrote them. Does he feel just a little bit responsible because he categorically refused to take me as seriously as I took myself? It would be nice to have someone to share some of the guilt with.

Well, that was Mrs. Klint. On whom shall I try my art of disguise now?

March Eighth

When the fire in the stove and the gas heater, which I'm always afraid is going to explode, have warmed the living room up a bit, it smells exactly as it does in summer. It's strange, it's as though we left the room just a minute ago—nothing has been touched. Don't understand that they haven't turned everything upside down and at least taken Nana's things away with them. There are dresses and makeup and her sewing basket; up here in the bedroom are her summer nightgown, which still smells of La Chamade when it gets into the warm room, and her swimming suit and beach robe.

I'm not feeling at all well today. I can't get warm even though I've pushed the table over to the fireplace and am sitting with my overcoat on and sipping from a bottle of (Danish) whiskey. My whole body is trembling, and I have scarcely any control of my fingers—they keep hitting the wrong keys and I'm too lazy to go back and make corrections. Why should I? One should be able to type with gloves on.

My nose is stuffed up, and I'm drinking some camomile tea I found in the kitchen. There isn't anything mysterious about my ailment— it has all the indications of turning into a good cold. One has to pay for changing climates without being more careful about changing clothing and keeping away from motorcycle trips in the cold. It was lovely, by the way—it reminded me of the first years when we had only the motorcycle and I had Nana behind me. She was a good passenger and never resisted when the cycle leaned into a curve, and she held her hands around my waist while her breasts pressed against my back. She was never afraid and got me to teach her to drive—she could even work the kick starter. I won't find anyone like that again.

I've brought some of her things down into the living room; I've put on her bathrobe between my all too thin clothes and the fur overcoat. Won't be easy for me to take off in a hurry with that upholstering. Unfortunately, the cold has closed up something in my ears again, which was also closed during the flight, but which opened with a small pop right in the middle of "Denmark, the light night slumbers now" the first evening, or was it the second?—no, it must have been the first. Otherwise, I try to keep my ears open, but I don't trust them any longer. I don't mean to be melodramatic, but my gun is lying with the safety catch off beside my typewriter and at night it lies by my bed. Who knows if I'll handle it as well as an air rifle? Doubt it, but it can at least be used to threaten with. I who've strewn guns around in my books! (Remember that I once posed a very decisive question to Colonel Boisen: Can a gun fire after it has been in water? He answered yes, and that was lucky because if he'd answered no I'd have had to rewrite several chapters.)

This morning I got a bad scare. I had gone all the way down to Brantebjerg and a little way along the water to the sand dune where we went swimming last summer. It has stopped snowing and the wind has been blowing a bit, so the snow has fallen off the trees. There was ice on the water piled up in large floes, and the sand was hard and good to walk on. I had the beach to myself and lay down a little while on the sand dune. But about that scare. On the way home I went by Forest Ranger Hansen's house (when Mrs. Klint can't recognize me, I'm not afraid of being recognized by the Hansens) and suddenly there's somebody standing right in front of me (it seems as if he wants to block my way) and he says "Hi" in Danish. Before I've thought at all, I've, God help me, also said "Hi" in Danish while I try to get around him. It was Preben, the somewhat retarded fellow who works for them, and I don't think he recognized me. He says hello to everyone, but now there's the chance of his going in and telling Mrs. Hansen that he has met a man with a beard and a fur overcoat on the road who said hi to him. Might it even be possible that he recognized me? That would be a fine irony if I was recognized by a retarded fellow. He yelled: "It's cold" after me and I turned around and answered, "I beg your pardon," but what does that help?—I had answered him in Danish. The Hansens and Mrs. Klint are in daily contact and I'm sure that I shouldn't stay here a moment longer.

I had a lot to think about on my walk. There's the future, but I put that off; although I know that I can't keep on living here much longer. There is My Big Project, and I feel the batteries recharging—there's another novel in me, and I am, so to speak, right in the middle of it. Finally, there's the question that arises terribly delayed: Whose is (was) the guilt? Who is the real murderer?

I hate novels where the guilt is thrust from the murderer onto society, the system, or what have you—something abstract. One is responsible, and if one doesn't have a God in heaven, then one is simply responsible to oneself. One can't share his guilt with a whole society. An unhappy childhood (and mine was happy) is no excuse, not even a real explanation. If one is going to share the guilt with anything, it has to be concrete; it has to be with another person, other people. I'm looking for someone to share the guilt with. Nana, whose scent rises to meet me from her beach robe, has her share in the guilt. I wonder why she married me in the first place, and I wonder when she was first unfaithful to me. Memories come surging in which I would rather push away. She goes in the morning to the TV center, and when I call to give her a message, I learn that she is not expected today. As time goes on, I get to know the girls at the switchboard, and I think they feel a little sorry for me or for their having fun at my expense. In the beginning there's always an explanation when she comes home—a filming was canceled and she went to town instead, or the girl at the switchboard must have been asleep at the switch because she *was* there and it's just that the girls didn't feel like looking for her. I argue that they said she hadn't even come in today, and she answers that so many people come in that they can't possibly know about all of them. If I press the point further, she asks me (I always fall back into the present tense) whom do I trust most, some incidental switchboard girl or her? Once I drove out there and after trudging a long time through halls and looking into studios and cutting rooms, I found her, it is true, in the canteen. But another time I didn't find her, and still she insisted when she came home that she had been there the whole day. Explained that everywhere I went they had said she wasn't expected at all today, and she said then she didn't understand the whole thing; she had been there the whole day, but perhaps had been in the toilet while I was looking for her, or had I perhaps been in there too?

One day last summer she was taking a sunbath when we heard a car approaching, and she put on her beach robe. The car crept in first gear (one of the sounds my deaf ears try to catch) up over the hill by Essmann's farm and drove up beside ours. When she saw it was her producer, Tom—they were preparing a program about hash—she took off her beach robe again and went to meet him. I'm not a prude, and we don't use bathing suits among friends up here, but the sight of Tom in city clothes and Nana without a stitch on (must soon begin cleaning up my language a little) embarrassed me. Later we drank tea and she got him to take off everything except a pair of striped shorts. After he had driven away again and I raised some objections, she said, Good Lord, we've worked together for years. She was manic about the sun and hated stripes. Got me down on that part of the beach where people swim without suits and walked a long time back and forth on the beach before she went in the water. My reaction was mixed, I can remember; there was something that excited me about seeing her in a thick cluster of naked men, and that day when Tom had gone I took pictures of her on her beach robe, and in the evening we made love in front of the fireplace as though in some sort of speculative film. God knows where the pictures are now. I don't think I ever finished the roll.

When it comes down to it, I think I am on the wrong track; if Tom had been one of them, she would have kept her beach robe on. Maybe she wasn't unfaithful to me at all (except the time we separated at a party and she admitted it afterward; good Lord, I've had too much to drink—I can't remember his name) until she told me about it and asked if we couldn't live with it until it passed over. But it didn't pass over—that is to say, it did, but not until after we were divorced—and I couldn't live with it. Could he do something I couldn't, and did they discover something together that we had never discovered? The paradox is that I am not monogamous either; I was quick to pay her back, but I couldn't help fantasizing about what they had together which we perhaps had never had. Maybe everything would have been different if we had had children, but on that point I knew what I was letting myself in for; she didn't want to and she had told me that honestly ahead of time. She wasn't afraid to give birth (although she didn't dare see *Rosemary's Baby*), but there were enough children in the world, she said, and she herself hadn't particularly enjoyed being a child (damn well wouldn't think so, with those parents). Or was it just that she didn't want me for the father of her child? She became completely impossible when I brought the subject up. (Reminds me of Shaw's reply: "Yes, dear lady, but suppose it was the reverse. Suppose the child got my beauty and your intelligence?")

One person alone doesn't bear the guilt, it can be shared; if it couldn't be, it couldn't be borne. The question is how many of us are in on it?—and here's where My Big Project comes in. I have a fever, it's true, but in the fever it begins to take form. I'm not sure that I can't use Bendix, Bang, Baxter, and several others after all. It will be my best book, the one L. wanted me to write, even if I have to learn to write with gloves on, because my fingers are stiff and my eyes are running and I can feel the whiskey whirling with the fever in my blood.

A sound made me go to the window, ease it up, and push open the shutters to look out. Someone is walking around the house whistling. It's Preben. When he's walked around a little, he goes whistling down toward the woods again. He has seen the motorcycle, and he has certainly also seen the smoke rising from my chimney. Now what will he tell the Hansens? Nothing, I'm sure. He doesn't say anything unless he's asked; his only contact is to pop up in front of someone and say hi. Nevertheless I ought to prepare a story in case they decide to come up here. Best of all, I ought to take off, but I don't have the strength for that; I can just see myself heading down the hills in the snow with a high fever and my necessities in my shoulder bag.

I stick the gun in my pocket. It shouldn't be lying around if they suddenly come to the door, but I have to have it ready if they recognize me.

March Tenth

Fever falling, and I'm at a stage in my cold where a succession of feelings in my mouth and throat put me in direct contact with my lost childhood. To have been sick and be on the point of recovering. To be fussed over, lie in languid euphoria, to relish your own receding cold and experience various visual disorders straightening themselves out and things around you moving back into their proper relationship to one another again.

There's no one to fuss over me, that's for sure, and for a few hours I was frightened enough to think I was going to die. I'm certain I had a fever of over 104 because I had hallucinations and daydreams. Someone tried to wrench the pillow from under my head in order to get hold of my revolver, and at one point I grabbed the revolver and aimed it threateningly out into the dark room—the last of the fire was about to die out, and I didn't have any wood left, nor the strength to go out and get some. It's just as well—the smoke from the chimney is a security risk. From now on I'll have to be satisfied with the warmth from the gas heater, but I'm afraid that the tank is nearly empty. Don't really remember whether in the middle of everything I fired a shot at the shadow figures which were gliding across the floor and up the wall to the ceiling, but I don't think so. I think the shot was just an echo in my head.

I was a frail child who liked to lie sick in bed. In a way, enjoyed submitting to someone else's care even when there was something more unpleasant the matter—for example, my appendix. I think the same thing manifested itself from the beginning with L.—I came and laid my situation in his hands and expected him to perform miracles. Sat across from him and expected him to do all the work. And when I didn't get rid of my depressions overnight, I began to pester him for prescriptions. I could use some now. I've run out of stuff to drink myself to sleep on, but that doesn't matter so much because the fever gives me long periods of sleep, though spread out very erratically over the twenty-four hours. My sense of time is completely confused; the only thing I know right now is that it's dark outside. The date I've put down is just a guess—it may be a day earlier or later. What I really could have used was penicillin and those codeine drops, which were my childhood introduction to euphoric drugs. Remember how when I had a cold I stole into the bathroom after everyone had said good night and took an extra swig from the bottle and afterward lay in bed and tingled with pleasure. L. says that I am *oral,* and I accept that from him with a big cigar in my mouth. He may be oral himself— he chain-smokes and inhales the smoke deep into his lungs.

In my delirium I dreamed I went hunting with Straus. We walked along the edge of the beach, and in front of us rose an enormous castle which belonged to Straus. In smooth transitions, Straus turned into my brother and back again (ah, how the pieces fall into place; I wouldn't want to tell this dream to L.—it's too easy. He should have something more difficult, although there is never anything that is really too difficult for L.). No, I didn't want to shoot him—we were reconciled. While we searched for prey, we made great plans for working in collaboration. Reached the castle, where a huge party was going on. Nana and my mother were stirring a kettle and handed each of us a steaming glass of something to strengthen us for our work. Forgiveness and reconciliation. My parents had at last reconciled themselves to the fact that I wrote about murder and blood. A siren broke up the party, and we all went down into the bomb shelter, where we listened to the bombers streaking in low over the coast. The sound changed as the guests disappeared, and Straus, whom I had embraced (here L. would be taking notes furiously), turned into air between my hands. Nearly awake, I realized that the noise of motors came from a car that was working its way up toward Baunebakke in low gear. Well, I thought, lying there with no plans for taking off, let them come and let's be reconciled. The car stopped, and the next thing I heard was doors slamming and a dog growling. Steps that came nearer, and someone trying to quiet the dog. Heard them call the dog. It was

Pasop, so it was the assistant forest ranger's jeep. Preben had gossiped, but had he told them, I wonder, that I had said hi in Danish when he said hi to me? To try to get away now was out of the question, and if they hadn't seen the smoke from the chimney, they had at least seen my footprints and my Tiger Cub all set to take off. Decided in my feverish fog to pretend not to be home, but when they had hammered long enough on the door, they simply pushed it open—I hadn't locked it the last time I was out.

Well, that's the end of it, I thought, but everything went better than I could have dreamed. I hurriedly took off my glasses and pushed my hair down over my forehead (should have thought of a wig), and they didn't recognize me. In the midst of the confusion, which wasn't lessened by the fact that they didn't understand my English and that my English was reduced to a confused minimum, I managed to explain—I don't know where the inspiration came from; I can be very inventive in emergencies—that I had rented the house from Nana's brother. I explained that I was a business acquaintance, had got permission to use the house, and now lay there in a fever. I think the only word that got through was fever. Mrs. Hansen spoke Danish with her husband, who was directing the proceedings, and wanted to bring up food and something warm to drink. Declined an offer to move down with them until I was well again. Just a little flu, I insisted. Behind them, Preben's face popped up—you can't tell by looking at him that he's forty; he said a cheery hi in Danish and was disappointed when I only nodded and said hello. Pasop wanted to get into bed with me—I nearly lost my head because I've always been afraid of dogs, and besides there was a kind of joyful recognition in his excitement—but Hansen held him back. No indication that they recognized me (in Nana's bathrobe!), but sooner or later they'll certainly call up Nana's brother, and before that I've got to take off. Or could I improvise my way through yet another emergency? The fever made me self-confident, and I spoke English for a long time (in my new voice, which wasn't made poorer by the fact that I was as hoarse as a raven) and even mustered enough courage to pat the dog. Without glasses and with a high fever, I felt strangely irresponsible. They conferred with each other for a long time in Danish, and since my cold had closed my Eustachian tubes again, I could only make out scraps of the conversation. Warm farewells with promises to return.

Later—it was still light—Mrs. Hansen and Preben came back with meatballs and potatoes in a plastic container and a bottle of malt beer and a thermometer. Got a brilliant inspiration and stuck the thermometer in my mouth! Which made Preben—who had tried once again with his hi in Danish—break out in a loud burst of laughter, while Mrs. Hansen took the thermometer from me, dried it with the towel by the washbasin, and with some embarrassment showed me how it should be stuck in before she left the room.

When she returned, I had shaken it down a little, because I don't want them calling a doctor. As I had expected, the thermometer registered nearly 104, but I shook it down to 100.4. Would have liked to ask for a bottle of whiskey, but I didn't want to see them again and continue the comedy act.

It is night—it must be the night between the ninth and the tenth of March. My disguise is a success: I haven't been recognized. People can't recognize me any more. First the taxi driver, who spoke English to me without thinking; then Mrs. Klint, who doesn't have anything wrong with her eyes either; then the Hansens. Strangely enough, I think Preben is the closest to recognizing me; there's a certain degree of irony in that. Now I'm no longer afraid to show myself; when the fever goes down I'll go into the city—I miss Copenhagen.

A wild idea: I could look up Mogensen or I could go over to Gyldendal. But on what pretext? No, first I'll just go into the city and stroll down the Walking Street and across the Raadhusplads.

It's about to get light out—six o'clock; it gets light earlier now. I've been out to take a piss. It's frosty cold and my breath freezes into small icicles on my mustache. Now I'll go in and sleep with all the pleasurable languor of childhood colds in my body, and before I fall asleep I'll think some more about My Big Project. But when my fever has gone down and I have perhaps added something new to my disguise, I'll no longer be afraid to go into my beloved Copenhagen, and who knows, maybe I'll pay a little visit.

The meeting with the Hansens has given me new courage.

March Twelfth

My body still racked with fever, I go down toward Bakkerne and take a bus to town, where I buy warmer clothes, boots, and a large scarf. In the window of the bookstore both my and Straus' fall books have disappeared; on the other hand, Straus' spring book is displayed in a huge pile: *Wedged Against the Wall.* It sounds—aside from involving the usual Strauslike alliteration—noticeably like my old article: "With Your Back to the Wall." The publication is being celebrated, as a matter of fact, this evening with the performance of a new Straus radio play: *Comic Strips Without Cartoons.* It sounds as though Straus is going to make himself even more "high class." Some people were whispering even last fall about the Critics' Prize. And then I recall that he has had a summer book and a TV series and a film and a fall book and undoubtedly some fifth thing in the works right now. One consolation: Helga has sold my books at least as well as Straus' in foreign countries, but neither of us has had many editions issued there, and I don't think it is necessarily an indication of quality that one can be exported. It is more likely due to the fact that one writes straightforwardly and simply—an attribute I've always refused to accept in myself because I know it's the most difficult thing in the world. Yes, I am fighting back today; it's easier to write in a complicated style.

On the train I read the reviews of Straus' new book. Boy, isn't he good? There are practically no exceptions to the enthusiasm. It seems as though a couple of the men have been in contact by telephone or some other way because exactly the same quite penetrating observations appear in two papers. Straus has written a documentary novel (I clearly remember the case) about a man who is pointed out by everyone in a small-town bank as a hold-up man who tried to empty the till. Straus is close to my idea about Bang's novel of a traveling salesman, because there are no witnesses and right in the middle of the whole thing the man's lawyer dies and his wife is admitted to the hospital with a severe case of depression. Then comes a surprise, which everyone regards as a new potential in Straus' authorship: the man goes down on his knees and prays to Jesus Christ for help, and a miracle occurs. The real criminal stages a new hold-up and muffs it. Our hero gets free, but the novel concludes in a mood of uncertainty because the wife is still sick and there is no promise that she will be cured. The reviewers are by and large agreed that the prayer is a real coup for Straus. It is not to be interpreted religiously; Straus hasn't suddenly turned religious, he has simply carried his view of society to its logical conclusion (yes, now Straus is definitely on a level where one has a view of society): In the complex machinery of society the little man has only one way out: the miracle. And precisely by letting one man be saved by a miracle, Straus tells us that the majority are lost because they can't hope for a miracle; once they get into a bind, they are hopelessly caught. A large picture of a laughing Straus in hunting costume in *Politiken,* which doesn't really go with the serious book; the review has as its headline STRAUS' LATEST ALTERNATIVE, and as a sub-headline: *With his spring book Straus takes the part of the helpless against the machinery of society and has perhaps written his best novel.*

I didn't dare to go in and buy it because it would look strange if I went in and asked in English for a Danish book. Besides, I've stopped reading Straus' books (I am reminded of my reply in an interview: I don't read, I write. And of the cartoonist Ingvar, creator of "Tjavs" and "Magasin Madsen", who had been in Paris and was asked why he hadn't been to the Louvre. He answered that he was afraid of ruining his stroke!)

At the Tisvilde Station I nearly got into trouble. A group from Nordic Films was in the process of sluicing snow away from the area around the station: they were going to shoot some film, and they had been waiting there in vain for the area to get clear of snow since November. Right in the middle of everything stood Balling directing the troops. Guess which film they were about to apply the finishing touches to. Well, I bought a copy of *Vogue* (the only foreign magazine I could find) and got into the train hiding behind that. But was very tempted to go directly over to Balling when he stood by himself for a moment with his handkerchief out, and ask in English: What's going on here? Sooner or later I have to make the test with someone I know that well.

In my feverish condition I have got quite a bit further with my plans for the future. I am thinking about my Project and I no longer see any obstacles in getting it published. There is something called *sending* one's manuscript to the publisher; that worked fine with my English and American publishers, and if I don't dare to go up to see Mogens Knudsen in my disguise, I could translate the book myself and try to get it published in English. Who knows, maybe translate it back into Danish! I could suggest myself as the translator! It's a wild plan and I'm putting it off until I have the fever completely out of my system.

Very mystified about what is hidden behind the title *Comic Strips Without Cartoons.* While we rolled through the North Zealand landscape, I guessed that Straus is flirting with pop art this time. My guess would prove to be right (decided to buy a transistor radio in town: I'm beginning to get tired of Schiøtz). In town I figured out a small improvement upon my disguise: you can get colored contact lenses now. So I no longer have blue eyes; they're brown. I was approached by a fag on the Raadhusplads and decided to be a little more restrained with my eye makeup in the future. Otherwise I've made very clever use of Nana's makeup materials, especially the eyebrow pencil.

It was cold frosty weather with just a little sun on the Raadhusplads, and I cut across it diagonally with my transistor radio to the Politiken Building and went in. Avoided Mogensen's route and just looked around a little. Got a beer in the canteen and read the day's *Ekstrablad.* Ten lines for Straus, who was taken to task for a change. Borum felt that Straus "in his eternal search for contacts with new readers" had "tried to make himself heard by his enemies in Vendsyssel with a little miracle." Also some comment that he "trampled Capote in his spinach bed" (I can't stand Borum's mixed metaphors). Well, the newspaper had immediately telephoned Straus and asked him about all the good reviews and the one poor one. "God, haven't I become godly," he said in the headline. Then there was a little about the radio play, and finally it was announced that Straus had sent his whole family to the Bahamas (our roads cross) in order to get some peace and quiet to complete a new novel. It must be the fall novel Knudsen spoke about. They had dug up the old pictures where Straus is writing on two typewriters at once.

I got out of the Politiken Building without being challenged and sauntered down the Gaagaden. Ate lunch at Cheval Blanc and looked at girls and shops. Down along Købmagergade, and down to Klareboderne. I took courage and went up into Gyldendal's anteroom, but then thought better of it and got out of there quickly. The girl in the anteroom looked at me a long time and asked me whom I wanted to speak with. I improvised (in English, of course) that I wanted to speak with Mr. Straus. When she suggested that I speak with Mrs. Lindhardt in the foreign section I became really afraid (*she* has sharp eyes, the local Mrs. Klint) and I think my exit seemed very strange. But what more can I do to be unrecognizable?

Took a taxi to the radio station (on all the unbeaten paths) and there things nearly went badly. After having looked around a bit, I ended up in the cafeteria with a cup of coffee and suddenly Tom was coming right toward me. I got up in panic, overturned a chair behind me, and hurried toward the exit. It was certainly the table next to me that Tom was headed for; but when I turned around in the doorway, he also had turned and was staring after me. He put down his beer and began (as far as I could see before I disappeared out of the door) to come after me. I hurried down the stairs, into a toilet, and locked the door after me. I don't know what would have happened if he had come in and begun to pound on the door, but when I had sat on the toilet for a little while and tried to get my pulse down to normal again, I unlocked the door and found a complicated route out of the building. And so homeward in the car I've rented (Anthony Baxter) with my new eye color and my new transistor radio.

The Hansens are no risk because they don't know Nana's brother and can't verify whom he has got it into his head to rent the house to. But Tom is a risk because he knows Baunebakke and he knows Nana's brother. I got stuck with the heavy-nosed Mercedes just below Essmann's farm, and since I had no desire for contact with more people that day, I didn't phone to Falck, but just managed to maneuver the car over to the edge of the road. I filled up the storeroom behind the kitchen with provisions and went into hibernation again.

Straus' radio play dealt with a murder at a Home for the Blind, but I've turned it off because I can't really follow it. I've drunk too much whiskey, and now I have to begin to listen for cars coming up the hill or steps near the house. I've taken far too great a risk today; I'll have to move soon and I must find a better disguise, but what?

Novel technique observation: the diary form isn't suited for suspense. Here I sit and write, and everyone can figure out that I have got through the day in one piece. Should I perhaps go back to my old friend Baxter, whom I became so fond of?

It's cold, but there's a bird singing in the twilight. Good to see all the old places again, but in the middle of everything something happened which I've forgotten again and I'm trying to recall. Something I did or saw which I ought to remember and keep in mind. What can it be? I'm too drunk to remember it; the day has offered too many impressions.

I'm thinking like crazy about a better disguise.

March Thirteenth

Struggled a long time with my car and finally got it out. It snowed last night, and someone has written WASH ME on the trunk lid, so there is obviously some form of life in the hills.

My car has rental-car plates, so I wasn't afraid to use one of the vacant parking spots at the British Embassy. I had already considered possible new disguises, but had rejected them all. I could shave my head bald, I could outfit myself with a wig, or I could dye my hair gray, but these things would just make me look more suspicious. My only get-up was a pair of extra-heavily drawn eyebrows and a touch of red on my lips (Nana's lipstick), which I thought would make me look a little more southern. (What about plastic surgery, what about a hooked nose, tight new skin under my eyes and maybe a tattoo on my arm?) I went up to see Fromberg after having introduced myself to the receptionist as Anthony Baxter and made sure on the way up that there were other ways out. My car was unlocked and (certainly a risk) the keys were in it so I could get away quickly. I had my revolver in my pocket—strange feeling to go into venerable old Gyldendal with a revolver in my pocket.

Fromberg sized me up so carefully (the lipstick was undoubtedly a mistake) that for a moment I was on the point of taking off, but then he offered me a cigar, and I dropped into the chair across from him. Explained that I had heard about my own case and represented an American publishing firm that was considering the possibility of writing a documentary novel about a crime writer who became a murderer himself. Fromberg explained, as I had anticipated, that this wasn't his department, and I said I more or less realized that—I was only doing research. Couldn't he explain a bit about myself? Had I seemed unbalanced?

After reflecting a moment, Fromberg said that I had been very interested in my sales figures and often telephoned to find out how my books were selling. I had written my own blurbs for the jackets of the books and had put a lot of effort into getting the jacket design worked out according to my own ideas. I always went to the book salesmen's meetings and gave a little pep talk to the salesmen before they went out to book dealers around the country to talk about my new book. I had the whole outline for my fall book in my head the previous winter, long before I'd started writing it. I appeared at Gyldendal even when I didn't have any particular errand and just came in to chat. I pressured them to publish my earlier books in paperback and in book-club editions, but I (Baxter) had better talk with Ringhof and Lindgren about that.

Had my murder led to new editions being published? No, their policy had been to stop sales; they weren't interested in cheap sensationalism. Did he have a statement of sales? Yes, my editions were sold out, but they hadn't begun new ones. Foreign sales? Yes, I had kept close track of that, but I had better talk to Helga Lindhardt about that. Had they found any trace of me? No, I had vanished without a trace. Then who received the money owed to me? That was a problem. A decision would have to be made in September when the payments fell due, but my brother-in-law had already applied for them.

What was Fromberg's own personal impression of me? That I was ambitious. But now the roles were reversed—he wanted to hear more about this book that was going to be written. Couldn't I talk with Mogens Knudsen? Was it necessary to rake up a case that the publishing company hoped would die down? Perhaps; I was, as I said, only here doing research. With the loaded revolver in my pocket, I left a somewhat bewildered Fromberg, who reached for a telephone the moment I stood up. Got out of the building in a hurry. I had the feeling that there would be a lot of telephoning going on in the next hour.

I've taken far too many chances. I have to be careful. My disguise stood its test, but I've aroused some suspicions that I'm not sure I can stop by just staying away from Gyldendal. It wouldn't surprise me if Baxter turns up in the newspapers tomorrow: an American wants to write a book about the crime writer who committed murder himself. Baunebakke is no longer safe, and my car isn't safe—I rented it in Baxter's name, and now there's the risk that they'll begin to look for it. The Hansens read the newspapers, and they'll certainly be able to put two and two together.

Returned the car on the way out of the city and rented a new one at another place under a new name: Bayle—lucky I had several passports made before I returned—Anthony (there my imagination gave out) Bayle. It was a Simca, and this car was able to drive all the way up to Baunebakke. No fresh tracks in the snow.

Yes, now they're making telephone calls. Baxter is in the city, and even if Baxter has returned his car and got out of sight, they'll certainly come after me. My brother-in-law will hear about the mysterious Mr. Baxter before the day is over, and then I can expect a visit at Baunebakke. I have to find a new hiding place, and I have to find a new disguise. I have to begin all over again. Luckily, I've got an idea —there's a busy evening ahead.

March Fourteenth

I think my constant writing in diary form has something to do with my need to communicate with someone. The diary is, of course, not designed to be read (although it becomes more and more a part of My Big Project—life is poetry), but I haven't had a good talk with a living soul in over two months now, and my need to talk to myself is beginning (wasn't there a hit song called "I Talk to Myself"?) to get out of control to such a degree that I'm afraid that after an exhausting day I'll borrow a typewriter from the porter, keep my neighbors awake, and in general play a lot of deadly dangerous comedies.

That's the distinctive thing about the diary form: that the sun *has* set; one knows the day. This morning I only knew that I had taken far too great a risk; I didn't know how close on my heels they were. And in fact the day began so well because my new plan was completely crystallized. Right after breakfast I went up to the bedroom and got out Nana's things. After having locked the door so I couldn't be surprised by the Hansens or Preben, I changed in a hurry. I kept on my usual underclothes, but pulled Nana's pantyhose over my shorts. Then her slacks, which were a little too short and a little too wide over the rear, too. But it was O.K.—there wasn't so great a difference between the two of us after all. I put her bra on over my undershirt (don't recall that she's worn a bra in years) and stuffed a little newspaper into the necessary places—I'll have to find a better solution for that. Over the bra and undershirt a pink sweater in order to make the whole thing a little more feminine. It was tight, but not so tight as to attract attention; I'm no muscle man and Nana wasn't

124

skinny. The fact that it didn't completely button in back couldn't be seen when I put a raincoat over it.

Then came one of the worst problems—the shoes. There was no way out of it, I had to use my own shoes, and none of them looked feminine. But there's an answer to everything; I noted on my tablet: Boots. Fur-lined boots are fur-lined boots, and you don't usually notice a few sizes' difference, especially if you choose a pair of decorated ones. But I was not presentable enough yet to drive down to town and buy boots.

I heated water, took out my electric shaver, and shaved my arms and legs carefully. Then I started on my beard—first with the scissors, then with the electric shaver as close as I could get. I was very careful because I didn't want to cut myself and go around with small cuts on my face. I ended up looking very strange because I'm winter-pale and Danish where my beard has shaded me from the sun. But I fixed that with Nana's makeup.

On the whole, the makeup was quite an operation. I had practiced for a long time doing various things with my eyes, but now I plucked my eyebrows with tweezers and put on eyeshadow. Put makeup over the pale parts of my face which my beard had covered, and put more rouge on my cheeks; followed the process with fascination in a little mirror which I had put up by the window (with wide-open ears for steps and the sound of a motor).

I had planned to cut my hair short, but decided it was so long now that it could pass for a woman's hair (I have "naturally curly hair"). It doesn't look like a woman's hair, but that can be arranged. Noted on my piece of paper: Carmen Curlers. As a finishing touch, tied one of Nana's kerchiefs around my head and wriggled with great difficulty into one of her summer raincoats; it was tight across the shoulders, but it will do. I don't know what sort of an inspiration made me pack the rest of her things in a suitcase and take out one of her large old purses and put all my papers and money in it, but perhaps I did that with a premonition that the Hansens might come up with new provisions for the sick foreigner. I even managed to correct Anthony to

Anthonya. I know very well that Anthonia would look more logical, but I didn't dare write over it. Then I drove (freezing because the raincoat is thin and the Simca's heater can't compare with the Mercedes') down to the town to buy boots and curlers.

In the car I practiced my new voice. It's not easy to pitch it higher when for several weeks you've been practicing to pitch it lower. The cold and my contact lenses, which I'll never get used to, made my eyes water, and I looked for my pants pocket, which I no longer have, for a handkerchief. Finally found a Kleenex in the purse and got that full of mascara because I rubbed instead of dabbing. There's a lot to learn, and I had to stop the car by the church in order to freshen up the makeup, using the little mirror on the sunshade on the passenger's side. So-called Madam's Mirror.

In town I found a shoe store and went in with pounding heart. Chose to speak English after all because I figured that that made the whole voice problem less dangerous. Returned to the car with red fur-lined boots—medium heel; was just about to lose my balance and fall over in the snow. I bought curlers in a supermarket.

I drove up to Baunebakke with a feeling I had better be careful now. The car nearly skidded on the icy road because it's difficult to manage the pedals with my new high-heeled boots. Carried on a long monologue with myself in order to practice my new woman's voice and thought at the same time about my passport and my international driver's license, where I have changed my name, it's true (profession still writer), but not the photographs. My premonition turned into absolute fear when I thought I noticed that there were more tracks in the snow than I remembered there should be. But there were no cars by Essmann's farm and I continued on—I had planned a couple more hours to complete the transformation.

From the top of the hill I immediately caught sight of a black Volvo parked among the trees in front of Baunebakke. There was no time to lose, and I backed lurchingly down the hill again. But now another Volvo had driven out and positioned itself in front of Essmann's farm, and for a moment I thought the game was up. I backed up hurriedly in between the trees so I got turned around the right way and steered down toward the Volvo as if I was going to drive in front of it. Made one of those turns where one is either lucky or unlucky and somehow or other slid on all four wheels past the car. And then down the hill as fast as I could.

I shouldn't brag about being a particularly good driver (I am) and I was neither particularly familiar with the boots or the new car, but one scurries around better on icy roads with a little front-wheel-drive car than with a big Volvo, and I got away from them. I had sort of expected that still another car would be waiting down by the road, but obviously they had sacrificed only two cars for the alarm, and that wasn't enough. Down on the freeway I turned to the right and thought as fast as I could. A Volvo is faster than a Simca, but it isn't good on icy roads even with snow tires and I didn't so much as see them in my rear-view mirror. Naturally they have a call radio, so I mustn't drive toward Frederiksværk. By Ramløse Creek I drove toward Helsinge, was tempted to take an empty taxi which was waiting in the center of Ramløse, but they have call radios in the cars, and I turned toward Annisse, where I pulled off to the side to think a little. Continued after a little while toward Hillerød, where I had a better chance to disappear in the everyday confusion.

Hillerød railroad station was a risky place, but I took the chance and hid behind a magazine in the waiting room (a new practice with my new voice: the ticket and the magazine). From the train window I got the last glimpse of my Simca and bade it a grateful farewell because it had helped me get away from two Volvos in the snow up in the hills. The police ought to consider a car that is better in rough terrain.

The woman's magazine *Eva* was full of good tips about winter fashions, and while I read it I discreetly brought my "breasts" into place; they had fallen a bit in the heat of the battle. Also took out my purse and fixed up my face a little. I had time to reconstruct the events and decided that Fromberg must have called Nana's brother, who then set the wheels in motion. They've been sluggish about the whole thing; otherwise, they would have taken me at the edge of my bed. Got off the train in Birkerød (didn't want to meet them at the main train station) and decided to venture taking a taxi. But first there was a problem I had already put off to the bursting point. The first visit in my life to a ladies' room.

Oddly enough, I was more exhilarated than afraid. Remembered to piss sitting down and *didn't* put the toilet seat up again when I left the toilet. Then a taxi to Lyngby station, where I remembered you could get a passport picture taken. Bought paste and a stapler in Lyngby and fixed up my passport and driver's license in a telephone booth before I took a taxi to the Hotel Marina. At two thirty Anthonya Bayle was registered in a room in the Hotel Marina, where she is sitting now and writing on hotel stationery.

Naturally they're now on the trail of a rented Simca, and naturally they already have the name Bayle from the rental agency. If they've been a little quick about it, they've begun to comb the hotels carefully. But did they realize in the flurry that there was a "woman" at the wheel? I can't stay overnight here. I have to move on, but first I have to put the pictures on my old papers and change my identity once again. Anthonya Baxter (have all the time really had a special affection for mysterious Mr./Miss Baxter).

"A new woman in ten minutes," it says on my curlers. It's really fun to be a woman. Mother once told me I should have been a girl, and that pink things were knitted for me when she was pregnant with me. She should see me now.

March Fifteenth

At last a day when I succeed in stealing the front page from Straus; but he isn't forgotten—there are articles about him inside the newspaper, and on the front page there's a page index to the two Straus articles, but I get the main headline today.

They've got most of it straight. They know I'm in Denmark, that I arrived as a certain Anthony Baxter on the fourth of March, and that I've lived in disguise (the Hansens' and Fromberg's description) in my own summer cottage—an unprecedented act of daring. A mysterious visit of a certain Mr. Baxter at Gyldendal's publishing house the day before yesterday aroused suspicion. Nana's brother became alarmed, and then the avalanche began. A little slowly, you would have to admit—a few hours sooner and I wouldn't be sitting here (in a Vesterbro hotel, where people are used to a little of everything and at least don't start asking you for your passport, not that I wouldn't have dared to show one after having read the papers all the way through).

The fact is that they've seen me disappear right under their noses (or, more correctly, behind their noses), but they haven't been sharp enough to note my new disguise—on the contrary, they make a big deal out of my having a beard, and the morning papers had time to get an artist to draw a beard on an old photograph of me (without making me long-haired at the same time, the clowns) and to further retouch the photo by removing my glasses, which didn't make me much more recognizable since my eyes remain small, as they were behind the strong glasses.

Otherwise, they've found out a lot. I left my typewriter and men's clothes and provisions at Baunebakke, but they haven't (or are they still holding something back from me to make me overconfident?) found out what I bought when I drove my Simca down to the fishing village just before the trap was to be sprung. They have found the car in Hillerød, but they haven't found out that I spent a couple of hours at the Hotel Marina and, with my heart in my mouth (as my heroes always had in my first books), got the last of my traveler's checks cashed there. There are pictures of the Simca—as if that would help with anything—and there are photographs of Baunebakke. Then there is a recapitulation of the whole case, and there are pictures of Nana and whatever else they've been able to think of. But there's nothing about my becoming a woman, and I feel more or less safe, because I'm becoming more and more a woman.

The articles on Straus are inside the newspaper. Rather poor timing for once, because if it hadn't been for me, he would certainly have been on the front page. There are protests from the Left and the Right, just what he always enjoys. Christian readers are indignant because he makes use of prayers and miracles in a crime novel, and then tomorrow the next team of readers will come to the defense of Straus' miracles. A spokesman for the Association for the Blind thinks that Straus is creating cheap sensationalism about a serious physical handicap, and tomorrow disconcerted readers will write in that Straus has taken up an important social problem and handled it seriously and honestly. In the meantime, the newspapers have telephoned Straus, and he willingly defends himself: He has used a miracle in order to show that the little man doesn't stand a chance when the machinery of society pushes him up against the wall. Straus is not religious himself (member of the Humanistic Society), and naturally he doesn't believe in prayers and miracles, but he just—ironically, if you will— wanted to show that a miracle is the little man's only chance. Aside from that, one can't run away from the Christian cultural heritage, and he is willing to meet his adversaries, preferably on television.

As far as the blind are concerned, he explains his radio play in the most beautiful terms. The idea is that the Home for the Blind is a symbol of existence. We are all blind—we have an expression "blind faith"—and all of us have to submit ourselves (Straus clearly has a religious streak, after all) to our fellow men, knowing full well that there may be a murderer at our side. The criminal intrigue is only an excuse for making a more general statement about the conditions under which we must live, and Straus is unhappy if anyone has got the impression that he wanted to ruthlessly exploit a handicap—here too the indications are that he's ready to discuss the matter.

Ekstrablad takes advantage of the opportunity to question Straus about his future plans. There are surely both a summer novel and a fall novel on the boards—can the veil be lifted a little? Straus replies that you shouldn't sell the hide before you shoot the bear, but he can divulge this much—his fall novel is a study in psychopathic jealousy. Some people will undoubtedly read it as a *roman à clef* because it is inspired by an actual event, but he has tried to make the theme universal. Which actual event? Well, just wait and see. But film rights are already being negotiated, and a Swedish company is interested.

The newspaper has dug up the picture of Straus sitting on a bagged elephant. Caption: STRAUS IS WAITING AWHILE TO SELL THE SKIN. . . .

In the back of the *Ekstrablad* I found an advertisement from a store that deals in something I can use. So now I have real breasts that don't fall down all the time, and after having given myself a very careful morning shave and cut my nails and polished them (an entertaining job) I dared go into a store and buy dresses that fit me better than Nana's. Have also bought false eyelashes and had great fun trying to get them to stay in place. Bought a wig and cut my hair in the room before I tried it on. It looks a little strange, but I have the scarf to conceal it until I find one that looks better.

Now it would be fun to talk with L. I'm sure that he would be able to figure everything out, but I'm not going to contact anyone else from my old life before I've considerably perfected my new role, if even then. My voice is the biggest problem; I practice pitching it higher while I fix myself up in front of the mirror. I'm always just about to go into the men's toilet and stop myself at the last moment. Also once in a while am about to fall over my own legs in the red boots with the medium heels, and after dinner today at the cafeteria I had a cigar halfway out before I stopped myself. Here in the hotel room I throw the butts out the window, which I keep open so the room won't smoke up too much while I'm writing. It's really funny to see the lipstick smears on the cigar butt before I toss it out the window.

I still lack the finishing touches, and meanwhile I walk around thinking of small improvements. Polish on my toenails, although no one will get to see them if all goes well. Have shaved the backs of my hands and bought filter cigarettes to smoke when I'm out. And a little woman's lighter that operates so stiffly I can hardly get it to work, using all the strength in my fingers. Oh, what women have to suffer for the sake of femininity. Ah, yes, and a watch, a silly little watch that I have to put right up to my eyes to see what time it says.

Men don't give up their seats for me in the bus, but they do turn and stare after me when I walk down Vesterbro Street at dusk. Also had to exchange glances that were angling for contact when a woman asked me for a light at the bus stop. Wasn't sure whether it was a real woman or not.

I remembered what it was I read too hurriedly in the newspaper up at *Politiken* the other day. I won't forget it again.

March Sixteenth

Women really have a hard time of it. After my first full day as a woman I have been lying sleepless and worn out for hours. To get my false eyelashes off was harder than ripping off a Band-Aid from the most sensitive spot—my real eyelashes somehow or other got mixed up in the paste, and finally it hurt so much that I had to soften the whole thing with warm water.

My pantyhose had worked themselves up pretty tight into my crotch, my knees were almost as tender as my feet from trying to maintain the peculiar balance on my boots, and my whole face itched. I didn't have any cold cream, and I thought you could get makeup off by washing enough, but the makeup turned into a strange viscous fluid which apparently seeped deeper and deeper down into the pores. After a couple of hours without sleep (the only help, a little Bols— I try to be a perfectionist) I had to get up and go to an all-night drugstore to get cold cream and Kleenex because I simply couldn't stand the way my cheeks and forehead were itching.

There's a sink in the room here, but no bath (I had to start thinking about economizing—my female outfit wasn't cheap), so I'd bought a nightgown and a bathrobe to wear to the bathroom. On the way to the bathroom (it was probably a little late to take a bath, and I can't allow myself to attract attention) I unconsciously whistled a melody, and it was only after I was lying in the bathtub that I realized what it was. How does it go now (pardon my French again)? "Quand tu prends, dans tes bras . . ." something or other, or maybe, "Quand *je* prends dans *mes* bras . . ." In any case it ends with: "Si petit. Si petit . . . si petit . . . si petit. . . ." It was quite a while before I realized where it came from. Danish Radio Theater (at that time it wasn't called Radio Plays). My brother and I listened to it in the maid's room. She had turned out the lights because it was supposed to be really scary, *The Murderer's Melody,* and in the middle of everything she presses my brother and me close to her, and it isn't just an ordinary embrace; I experience it as a caress of an entirely different intensity from that of my parents, and I know (the little spy) that it isn't just my brother and me that she is pressing to her—it's a man whom she's engaged to but who almost never appears (later it turned out that he had a good reason—he was a member of the resistance movement and turned up on the evening of the fourth of May with a confiscated Mercedes which my brother and I got a ride in; the maid in the meantime had got sick and had died in the hospital).

After my bath I lay thinking about *The Murderer's Melody* and about all the other radio plays we listened to with our maid in the dark that last winter of the war. Straus had one of his usual good ideas: one is blind when listening to radio theater—an excellent idea to have a radio play about the blind. When I got so involved in my job of turning myself into a woman, it wasn't because of anything L. would immediately think, and I reminded myself of how even that winter— the last before the liberation in 1945 when I was ten—was clearly taken up erotically with our maids; that braced me up. I also happened to recall how a maid had let me play with her jewelry, but all that has to do with my enjoyment in dressing up, playing roles. I am not a transvestite, I am just a perfectionist (the more I protest, the more L. makes notes in his little book). Nevertheless, my fate and My Big Project depend on my playing my role as well as possible. I have therefore perhaps exaggerated a little. I should have waited with the nail polish until my nails were long enough to file. And what a job it was to put it on the nails of my right hand. I'm not sure how you do it, and I couldn't find anything about it in the women's magazines I bought: do you paint the half-moon or do you let that stay un- painted? Out of my bed in the middle of the night and took all the nail polish off again.

The smell of the cigars made the air in the room difficult to breathe, and I'm not used to the sound of a rumbling city outside the window. Dozed a couple of hours and had one of those dreams where I go through a myriad of transformations and people and places around me drift and drift the same way. I was the observer of a tender scene between my brother and the maids somewhere—it must have been Baunebakke, but suddenly I had assumed the maid's role, and my brother had turned into Straus, and we found ourselves on the beach with a transistor radio while my parents watched us, smiling. Drifted back into the role of an observer while I was replaced by the black girl, whom Straus ended up choking (the last image before I woke up). Previously Tom had been part of it, and the black girl had turned into Nana. Straus strangled Nana, but not before he had partially undressed her and, among other things, had taken off her hair (wig). Meanwhile L. hovered around our little group and, squatting, made notes furiously. Awakened soaked through with sweat and didn't dare to be alone in the room.

My nighttime walk as a woman took me through parts of Vesterbro that I didn't know. It's finally begun to snow, and the streets are wet, with small piles of dirty melting ice along the curbs. I passed porno shops with lonesome people looking in the windows, and in my sleepiness and Bols-befuddlement I bumped into dark shadows. I ended up at Halmtorvet and was suddenly just as afraid to be here as to be alone. A man spoke to me:

—You don't want to go home alone, *do* you, Miss?

—Yes.

And when he positioned himself right in front of me:

—Get out of my way.

I had the gun in my purse and considered using it to frighten him when I wasn't able to shake him off, but tried another solution.

—I'm not any miss.

—No.

—I'm not even a woman.

—I realize that perfectly well. Come on, let me offer you a little drink, and we'll get things figured out.

In order to get away from him, I went out into the street and was nearly run over by a car which braked quickly to a stop. There was a woman driving, and she opened the door.

—Jump in.

I had already noticed the car, which had circled the square for a long time, but in order to get away from my pursuer I got in beside her.

—We're having a little party which you're welcome to join, she said after we had driven a little way and the man had given up running after us.

—Thank you, but if you will just let me off up on Vesterbro Street.

—I don't drive for free for a strange . . . man. Come on, now—you'll be taken care of, don't worry.

It cost me a fiver to be let out again without trouble. Which all goes to show that I can't be too careful—my perfectionism is not in the least overdone. In the car I'd given up using my woman's voice. In any case, that still needs a good deal of practice.

Trudged sleepily up and down Vesterbro Street while the city emptied and the neon lights were turned out. Now I sit writing long after midnight because I don't have anyone to talk to. The rest of my bottle of Bols I've poured down the sink—it won't do for me to be groggy when I wake up tomorrow. I'm putting off sleep until I know it will be so heavy that there won't be any room for dreams in it.

I put my typewriter on top of today's newspaper in order to muffle the noise. I'm still on the first page, but inside the newspaper the war rages against Straus, and it is announced that his third edition is on the way (they always cheat at Gyldendal with Straus' editions: they divide the first one into two). They haven't come one bit further with me. No, actually they've succeeded in finding L., but they don't mention him by name, simply that I was a patient of a well-known Copenhagen psychiatrist, and that he hasn't been able to give the police any information (they had certainly already contacted him in January).

The day's encouraging sign: I am taken out of the regular bookstore windows, but in the small secondhand stores I am in the windows and listed at high prices. When My Big Project is brought to completion,

135

the prices will be guaranteed to take a new leap forward. I shall make sure that I am not forgotten.

March Eighteenth

As part of my plan I've gotten a tape-recorder, a handy little one that can be carried in a woman's purse, but I'm afraid to use it; the walls are thin here—I have to whisper. The author of the future will work with a tape-recorder or a dictaphone. Straus disclosed in one of his innumerable interviews that he had recorded his entire radio play *Comic Strips Without Cartoons* on a tape recorder in order to hear how it came across in an audio medium.

Sitting here late at night whispering words into the tape-recorder, with whiskey and cigars too easily within reach, I'm well aware that there's something "wrong"—it would "help" if I could talk with someone; but I can't talk with anyone, and most of the "help" I can think of would be recommendations to give myself up, as if one automatically brought oneself back to some sort of innocence by surrendering, and I'm not even sure that it's innocence I'm looking for—it is justice.

I would like to talk with L., all his "systems" notwithstanding. It would have to be without my woman's costume, because that would throw him completely off the track and in a flash we'd be back to my childhood again, analyzing how it was with . . . Oh, well, he has always searched high and low for the failings of masculinity in my psyche—at the same time assuring me that *all* people are sexual composites. If I talked to him, it would be about the question of guilt, and I don't think I could get him interested in that at all. He, like all psychiatrists, wants to normalize me; he is normative, but he doesn't understand that for me the way to normality goes through justice. His norms are those of society (the happy family man with a little vice: smokes too much for his bad heart), just as mine have always been, but they can't possibly be my norms again until I've got justice.

I could look up Tom, but for Tom too I'd be only a case that should be solved, and at the same time it would reinforce him in all his theories. Namely, that my need for normality has made me crazy, that I'm a product of competitive society, and that I . . . and it's not unlikely that he'd hand me a pipe of hash and a red, and would then try to get to a telephone because he didn't dare take the responsibility for letting me run around loose. But for him the diagnosis would be clear: bourgeois society's rat race from the first months of life and all the way through school and puberty, until here I sat—the inevitable expression of dying bourgeois individualism, individualism run amuck.

I don't feel that any of that is *entirely* wrong; therefore I've never found a political "position." My "socialism" was dishonest—"pragmatic," I called it in interviews. In the first place, I never shared my money, although I went on hating the rich as I had done when I didn't dream that I might get rich myself; and in the second place, I couldn't get rid of the sportsman in me—he who wanted to be first across every finishing line. Characteristically enough, I've never been able to collaborate with others—I turned manuscripts in to my directors that were as explicit and complete as I could make them, with italics indicating what words the actor should stress and panorama and close-up shots painstakingly marked.

A journalist from a Finnish newspaper hunted me up after Nana had left, and we very rapidly got away from the usual questions. She was a convinced "liberated" female and naturally wanted to convince me too. Feelings of guilt and jealousy were rudiments of Christianity; the de-Christianized person would be freed from jealousy and guilt feelings—she had freed herself. I said that animals at the zoo show jealousy, and she replied that it was precisely because they were animals—civilization consisted in freeing yourself from all irrationality. I talked about my parents, whom I felt I'd neglected during that time when I should have reciprocated all the love they had shown me as a child, and she patiently explained to me that the only rational form of guilt feeling was the feeling of guilt over not having done what one wanted to. Finally, I got irritated and said that without my rudimentary feelings of guilt or jealousy I couldn't have written my books. She answered no, I probably couldn't have, and that the society of the future would probably find my books very strange. Did she want to get rid of all art? No, but bourgeois art would have to work at rendering itself superfluous by portraying phenomena like guilt and jealousy as rudiments from which people had to liberate themselves in order to be happy. She was, like all people who try to instruct me, a little bit crazy, but I couldn't help admiring her consistency. Next on her list was—guess who—and I really would have liked to be there with a white stick in my mouth when Straus explained to her about his miracles and his blind people, who quite irrationally trust their neighbors completely in a Home for the Blind where there is a murderer on the loose.

Straus has a private telephone number, and, on the point of leaving, she asked me if I could help her get it. I gave her good advice, which today I followed myself. Dressed in my best female clothes, I ventured up to the *Politiken* offices and, in an unobserved moment, slipped by the editors' receptionist and into the main editorial office. You just have to act as though you belong there. I said "Hi" to a solitary editorial assistant, and he said "Hi" in return and continued writing his article. On an unoccupied desk I located the newspaper's list of telephone numbers, and there was Straus' number with a little parenthesis after it (PRIVATE). Memorized it, and then quickly got out of the building again.

On the point of leaving (I'm giving up varying my word choice— just used that phrase, I know), I'd like to write a little about Nana. But I'm tired, and my typewriter will no longer do what I want it to. If I began all over again, I'd make more out of her, but it's too late to begin all over again. Straus is right—I only sniffed at her, I never really smelled her. When she realized she was going to die, it was as if she had already got used to the idea—she wasn't really panic-stricken. I'll remember her as she got out of the bathtub, a brief moment when she gave me the illusion of being happy, although I think she had just come from a lover. L. would never believe that I really loved her—he thought the problem wasn't to find someone who loved me, but to find someone I could love. But he was wrong. I loved Nana in my own way. For L. she was a "deviant" because she didn't want to have children, but L. had to fit everything into a system; and even if I believe we would have been happier—and everything could have been different—if we had had children, Nana isn't the guilty one. The guilty one is still walking around free.

Objectively, of course, I've gone crazy, but see how sensibly I'm writing. There's very little that remains to be done, and I'm acting perfectly sensibly, and I can no longer see how my plan can possibly fail. I've made the final preparations.

The phone conversation (from a telephone booth) went smoothly. Straus himself answered the phone; I introduced myself as a Spanish journalist, and he was all set to be interviewed immediately. I knew that Helga had sold *Stay out of Sight* to a Spanish publisher, and the interview was arranged in a moment—it would have surprised me had it been otherwise.

The final preparations are made. I have a cream that removes beard growth better than any amount of shaving, and the wig now fits so well that I'll be able to manage without the scarf. I've rented a car for tomorrow and put the cork in the whiskey bottle—it won't do for my hands to shake. The revolver lies in my purse, loaded, with the safety catch on. I'm going for an evening snack with Straus.

March Nineteenth

Splendid to be sitting at an I.B.M. typewriter again. Straus' is red, not olive-green like the one I started writing these notes on, but the typing element operates on the same principle: it twirls around and across the paper with movements too quick for the eye to observe and with a minimum of vibration. The way the ball turns around when you shift to capital letters is a fascinating little trick to watch, and it's a pleasure to see the whole typing element sail back from right to left when one line is written and a new one is to be started.

Straus understood how to organize his large worktable ergometrically or ergologically, or whatever it's called. The distance between table, chair, and typewriter is correct, and there are actually two typewriters (the other also electric, but the old-fashioned type) on the large Oregon-pine table, so you can sit down and roll your chair from one to the other, between manuscript and manuscript. On the table between the two typewriters is a thermos of coffee, and beside it a pack of Gauloises; a stack of white $8\frac{1}{2} \times 11$ paper is lying in a woven basket, and farther back on the table are piles of books and manuscripts. On top of one pile lies a red folder without many pages in it yet, on which is carefully pasted (it's much more orderly here than I had expected) a sticker with the words, BANG, YOU'RE DEAD!

I have to get a bit accustomed to the typewriter's hum, which discreetly reminds me that it wants to be written on. There is a white intercom on the table; I have unplugged it. The walls are covered with books, but in the place where my own should be (we exchanged books to the very end) there is a hole. My books, with the old dedications on the flyleaves, are stacked in front of the typewriter. Straus wasn't lying to me.

There is a stereo system here—which doesn't impress me—and a nice little collection of records, a small Japanese TV set that can be moved around at pleasure, a neat dictating machine, and a large tape-recorder. On a wall hangs a tourist poster for Ceylon and a large blow-up of a photograph of Straus and his family.

There is an adjoining kitchenette and a stall shower, and there is a sofa where you can lie down and think. In front of the sofa is a low table where an evening snack for two is laid out. I've downed the two cold beers, but the marinated salmon is still untouched. There is no sound here other than the hum of the typewriter and the dripping of melting snow in the misty park outside. I have opened the drapes and am looking out into the dark. When you stare out for a long time, you can distinguish the outline of the frozen lake.

Hans Christian Andersen once worked here, Straus told me with a wry smile, or grin, rather. Andersen visited the estate a couple of summers, and since he couldn't tolerate the disturbance caused by a couple of mischievous children, this house in the garden was fixed up for him. Straus had it restored and modernized a few years ago when he moved in. Legend has it that the famous sculptor Thorvaldsen has also been here, but Straus let matters go at hanging a small engraving of H. C. Andersen between the doors to the kitchen and the shower.

On the table in front of me are a pipe rack, with a pipe for each day, and a row of cans containing various mixtures of English tobacco. Among the tobacco tins are a bottle of headache tablets and a bottle of Noludar, one to two tablets at bedtime. Lined up carefully alongside each other are a speed-marker and a red, a blue, and a black ballpoint pen. An extra type-ball and a set of typewriter-cleaning tools are lying in a small dish. There is a rack for holding manuscripts that slides above the typewriter so you can do translations without having to sit with your head turned sideways over an open book all the time.

The coffee in the thermos is still warm. I've poured myself a cup and am writing calmly. I've taken off my wig and laid it on the table in front of me; the revolver is lying out because I have to finish writing this; there is very little left to write, and I'm not tired. It's been a difficult day. I've gone around waiting (with a dull feeling of being really out of it) after a night of short, disturbing dreams (I won't bore you by beginning to tell about them again), but I was never in doubt, and now I feel a relief that's been denied to me for months. I haven't eaten today, my hands couldn't have held a knife or fork, but I'm still not hungry. When I've written this, perhaps I'll go over and eat one of the two salmon sandwiches that are on the table.

I drove south out of the city after it got dark. I drove carefully because now it was more important than ever to avoid an accident and not get involved in anything. The weather was thawing and the roads were wet. I won't deny that I was tense. There was a sign in the village indicating the way to the estate, and I pulled off to the side of the road so I wouldn't arrive too early. I turned in to the tree-lined avenue of the estate; there were no lights in any of the windows. Approximately halfway up the avenue there was, as Straus had explained to me, a small road off to the right and I turned in to that. I could hear Straus typing inside the cabin, and first I went to the window and looked inside. There he sat at the typewriter—where I am sitting now—working away industriously. He uses the touch system; he was looking straight ahead through the dark window as if getting inspiration from the lake outside. He had a pipe between his teeth, and once in a while he broke off his writing to relight it with a table lighter that is still lying here by the typewriter. After studying him for a while, I knocked on the door.

I've made some dilettantish attempts to describe Straus. He is big, but very light on his feet. His face can appear dead, but you need only to look in his eyes for a moment to see that there is life there. I pretty much give up on describing Straus; one must try to imagine him for oneself (black turtleneck sweater and checked trousers with a suggestion of bellbottoms). As he looked deep into my eyes, I introduced myself in English, and he asked whether it had been difficult to find the way. Then he explained about Hans Christian Andersen and Thorvaldsen while he turned his back to me and went into the kitchen to get whiskey and soda. He put the bottles on the table, but remained standing with his back to me a little longer than I had counted on. There was obviously a bottle cap he couldn't get unscrewed. I stood with my purse in my hand, having no plans. The first move had to come from him, and it came too, but not until he had given up trying to get the cap off. Without turning around, he said in Danish:

—Well, so you've come to visit me.

I hesitated a little before I gave in and answered:

—Yes.

He still hadn't turned around, but had bent down slightly over the bottles.

—Oddly enough, I'm writing a book about you right now.

I had foreseen the possibility that he would recognize me before I took action, but I hadn't thought he had such sharp eyes. I drew the revolver out of my pocket, released the safety catch, and aimed it at him.

—I'm perfectly aware that I mustn't try to go over to the intercom; anyway, they're all sleeping up there now. Can't we sit down and have a talk together over a drink?

142

—Certainly.

He turned around and stared calmly at my revolver. One of the things I had thought about on the way down was that Straus the hunter undoubtedly had guns in his house, but I couldn't see any. Straus was thinking as rapidly as I was.

—I have a couple of rifles here in the cabin, but they aren't loaded, and I'm not going to make any attempt to get hold of them. Come and sit down so we can talk.

I moved closer, and he mixed two drinks and pushed one of them across the table to me.

—Do you have to point that thing at me?

I nodded, sat down facing him, and took hold of my glass with my left hand.

—Skaal, and welcome home. Oddly enough, I've dreamed about you every night since I heard you were back in the country. Are you thinking of shooting me?

I nodded.

—Listen, I have a suggestion. Couldn't we write that book together? I could hide you here, and we could write the book together.

—I'll write the book myself.

Straus took a sip from his glass. He was thinking now.

—I really don't want to die yet. There's so much I'd still like to write.

I didn't want to shoot him right away. I wanted to talk with him first, but I hadn't been prepared for the turn the conversation was taking and couldn't think of anything to do but keep on pointing the revolver at him.

—You regard me as a sort of accomplice, don't you?

—Yes.

—And if I tell you that I feel the same? We're in this book together.

—Yes, but I'll be the one who writes it.

—I could get it published. You'll never get a book published again.

He took a swallow from his glass and leaned back in the sofa.

—I don't want to die, you see.

—But you are going to die, Straus.

—I suppose I will. It was the review, wasn't it?

—That was just the straw that broke the camel's back.

—You realize that you're crazy?

—Yes.

—I'm about to go crazy myself. We have an acquaintance in common, let's call him L. We ought to join forces, we who are about to go crazy. What was it your book was called? *In the Same Boat?* You know, we're in the same boat. We ought to stick together.

—Yes, we're in the same boat, Straus. That's why we're both going to die.

—I had to be honest. I said what I really thought that evening on the radio. I had to say what I thought: I am number one and you are number two. But they're after us, they're after both of us. They're coming in swarms and they want air, they want to exist themselves. They're out after both of us.

—They're not out after me any longer.

—We're getting older; things can't go on like this much longer. Couldn't we write the book together first?

—It's my book. You won't get it away from me.

—You're a sick man. Give me that revolver now, and let's talk about what we can do with you.

—Straus, I want you to understand that you're going to die. That's why I haven't pulled the trigger yet. I want to give you time to understand. Think about it carefully, Straus; in just a little while you won't think any more. Think about death.

—I don't think about anything else. I think about it all the time. But there's still so much I want to accomplish. Listen, I'll accept my share of the guilt; we'll divide it. We'll divide it, and write a book about it together.

He had lost his composure; he couldn't hold the glass any longer and put it down on the table before leaning back against the wall. The man against the wall.

—We could be friends, he said. I've thought that we ought to be friends.

Now he was afraid, and that was all I'd wanted. Now he was human, now I knew what would come next.

—I've got a wife and kids. I don't want to die.

I put my glass down and aimed at his heart, steadying my right hand, which was shaking, with my left. I wanted to be sure that the first shot hit its mark.

—Well then, *skaal,* he said and leaned over the table, lifted his glass, and took a big gulp from it. I pulled the trigger, hitting his arm so that the glass broke, and he fell back on the sofa. I had shot very accurately; I think I hit him right in the center of his heart. He tried to get up, but fell back and made no further attempt to move. I remained sitting there until I was sure that he was dead.

Straus is a book which is guaranteed to keep its readers awake, not only at night but during the day too. It is a masterful study of jealousy and persecution mania, ingeniously composed so the reader never dares to decide completely where reality ends and fantasy begins. Furthermore, it happily avoids falling into the category of a glib psychiatric case study or the kind of facile social criticism which, in one quick sweep, reduces man's vague irrational instincts to a question of our sick society. The reader must keep his eyes and ears open, for the novel teems with hidden allusions that tie his entire authorship together in a new and convincing unity. With *Straus,* the crime novel has definitely reached its maturity. It is a book that deserves many readers and will richly reward them. . . .

The author has examined his own life with unprecedented courage, but his book is not exhibitionist—its theme is all too ordinary for that. The novel will be read as a *roman à clef,* but it is not, because we all have a Straus within us; even Straus himself surely has his Straus. The author has constructed his book with consummate skill for holding the reader's attention, but he never sacrifices his primary aim for the sake of cheap effects. One can imagine that writing this book was a colossal and perhaps also painful cathartic process, but at the same time this catharsis gives promise of an entirely new loftiness and liberation in an authorship that was perhaps on the verge of becoming rigidly routine. At the same time, the book is a caustic complaint against a society that forces individuals to a point where the drive for public recognition is so powerful it becomes an illness. *Straus* is a case study of competitive capitalistic society in all its ugliness, written so entertainingly that one reads it at a single sitting. . . .

Straus is a study of the sick mind, written with nerve endings attached to the typewriter keys; quickly read, slowly forgotten. It would be a pity to disclose the many sophistries and surprises along the way, but they are not the main thing anyway. The main thing is that the author forces us to a confrontation, if not an identification, with a sick man, and, shaken, we must acknowledge that we are all ill. We are civilized human beings with a thin shell of normality which protects us until chance tears the shell away and we must nakedly admit that we are all mad. Like all good doctors, the author has sweetened his bitter pill, but it *is* a bitter pill nonetheless, and we are wise to swallow it for the sake of our own health. . . .

Straus is a novel that finds its models where it can. In its complicated composition, where layer upon layer is exposed and the point of view is turned like mirrors which mirror still other mirrors, the book is perhaps reminiscent of Nabokov, but at the same time its tense forward-moving criminal intrigue with all the concomitant moments of excitement owes a debt to the classic suspense novel. Its diary form builds upon a long tradition in Danish literature; nor have the possibilities of the *roman à clef* been overlooked by the author. The amazing thing is that he has blended all these elements into a completely original work of art whose parallel is not to be found in modern Danish literature. Our film producers must be itching to be the first to get a share in it. . . .

Straus it said on the cover of the book, and I must admit that I opened it without particular enthusiasm. The commentary on the jacket did not sound promising, either; readers should know that it is with great skepticism that I approach crime novels which are too refined to be exciting and too intent upon being exciting to take themselves really seriously. Let me say immediately: this time my skepticism was put to shame, and I am willing to reconsider an entire authorship. *Straus* is a great book, greater than we are used to seeing published in our little Denmark. It is a book which makes one wise about oneself. I say without further ado: this book has filled me with unrest. We have many people in this country who write books, but we do not have many authors. The word suddenly takes on new meaning as I write it: individuals who have special knowledge to pass on to us. We have a new author.

Since Straus' death he is the greatest.

74 75 76 77 10 9 8 7 6 5 4 3 2 1